# TOXIC BEHEMOTH

David Bernstein

# CHAPTER 1

*Midnight in Brooklyn.*

The warehouse district along the Hudson River was like a ghost town, save for the multitude of rats and cockroaches that took up residence below and within the grime-layered and filth-encrusted structures. The rain came down in sheets, pelting the warehouse roof with a rumble that made Michael think the precipitation was laced with stones. He had no idea what was going on, but knew that waking up tied to a chair was not a good thing. A low-hanging, cone-shaped light shined from directly overhead, encompassing him in a circle of light that extended six feet out in all directions. The rest of the place was shrouded in shadow and he was barely able to make out his surroundings, but he knew he was in some kind of warehouse. He could just make out the stacks of crates and barrels along the walls. The air had a musty, mixed with saltwater odor to it.

Michael was a good-looking man. He had a slim build, stood just over six feet tall and had piercing blue eyes that held a person's gaze. His jet-black hair lay slicked back over his dome and the one-inch scar along his right cheek gave him an intimidating quality that fit his profession, almost making him appear even more handsome in a dangerous way.

His head throbbed where he'd obviously been clobbered. The last thing he remembered was being picked up to go to a meeting with *the boss*, Mickey Samson, a meeting he had been wired by the feds for, as part of his prison-avoidance and relocation deal.

Two months ago, he was stopped in his Mercedes after someone had called 911 and reported a man driving a Mercedes with his license plate number and fitting his description pointing a gun at other vehicles. After his vehicle had been searched, the cops found a .45 hidden under the passenger seat.

A ballistics test was performed. The weapon had been used in the murder of Frank Nicholas, a downtown lawyer known to have ties with organized crime. Of course, it was true, because Michael was the guy who killed Nicholas with a single shot to the back of the head.

But he'd gotten rid of the weapon. He'd given it to Vinnie, the boss' son. At the time, Michael thought it odd that Vinnie had wanted to dispose of the weapon, but he handed the piece over anyway.

After every hit, the weapon he'd used was always discarded. He would either toss it into the Hudson River or melt it down. Michael always took care of his own weapon disposal, needing to know that it was taken care of properly. When Vinnie had asked for the .45, Michael hadn't been prepared for such a thing and was caught off guard, something that rarely happened to him. But who was he to argue with the boss' son—the man who, one day, would run the family business. Besides, he had thought at the time, no one was going to find Frank Nicholas' body.

The corpse had been tossed into the cement foundation of a high-rise building going up in lower Manhattan, never to be discovered. Unfortunately, the cement mix hadn't been up to code. Cracks formed and the foundation had to be replaced. Frank Nicholas' body was discovered intact with the bullet inside the skull. The finding never made the news, the cops keeping the fact that they had a semi-preserved corpse and bullet to themselves, just in case the shooter had been foolish enough to keep the gun.

As soon as the weapon had been found in his car, Michael knew he'd been set up. He recognized the weapon when the cop showed it to him, a .45 Sig Sauer painted a dull black, the serial numbers having been melted off with acid.

It had to be Vinnie who had set him up, he thought, hence the reason the man had wanted the gun. Two plus two always equaled four. He should've been more careful, insisted he be the one to get rid of the weapon.

Michael had no idea why he'd been set up, but it was clear his days of working for the Samson family were over, and he wasn't about to spend the rest of his life in prison, apart from his wife and children. So he decided to make a deal.

He didn't like ratting. Never had ratted. Never shared secrets with others that he was told in confidence. He was a standup kind of guy. Rats deserved death. But on this occasion, squealing was justified, because his employer's son had broken the code first. He wouldn't give up the old man. Michael was sure Mickey had nothing to do with the set up. Therefore, he made the deal to get Vinnie, who was the next in line to take over the family business anyway, assuring the feds that Vinnie would roll over on his father in seconds. Vinnie was a coward and a loud mouth who liked to talk, hence the wire Michael was wearing.

While he'd been in holding, awaiting a visit from the feds, Michael wondered why Vinnie wanted him put away. Why not just kill him? The only thing he could come up with was jealousy, and that rotting away in prison was far worse than meeting one's maker.

Michael was close to Vinnie's father, and Vinnie was a screw up. Nevertheless, being the boss' son, Vinnie had power and would one day become boss—if he wasn't killed first. This allowed the crazed weasel to do as he pleased. Others feared him, knowing when he took control, things would change, and everyone wanted to be on his good side. Plus, he was certifiable, like the time he'd killed a bodega owner for short-changing him fifty cents.

Michael should've known something was up at the time Vinnie had asked for the murder weapon. He should've refused to hand the gun over. It hadn't felt right, but he ignored his gut. He would've gotten shit from the man, but it would've been worth it over the shit he was in now. He could've kept an eye on the psycho, taken him out quietly if he thought the man was gunning for him.

Of course, hindsight is always 20/20, as the saying goes, and he was facing a murder charge now, which meant freedom by the time he was an old, feeble man, or worse—he would spend the rest of his life in prison. And if he ratted, which no one thought he ever would, Vinnie would have the right to have him killed.

Michael figured his best course of action was to go straight, make a deal. He figured, even if he didn't sing to the cops that he'd be killed in prison. Hell, Vinnie was a nutcase, and Michael was afraid to leave his family unprotected. He had a wife and two kids to think about. He'd made bad decisions, led a dangerous life, but things changed. It always came down to the individual and his family, and that's what he decided to protect when he decided to rat.

Once the feds got wind that Michael wanted to make a deal, they swooped in like hungry jackals. They wanted the old man, Vinnie's father, a notorious mob boss that had eluded prosecution since he took power of the family over twenty years ago—the witnesses always disappearing or recanting their stories. They would get him by getting to Vinnie.

Michael agreed to wear a wire and gather information. In exchange, he would skate on the murder charge and enter the witness protection program with his family, including his wife's mother. Along with prosecuting the old man—Vinnie's doing, should he rat out his father—Michael wanted the feds to make sure Vinnie was sent away and could in no way escape prison time. He wanted assurances that there would be no deals or witness protection for that scumbag. Of course, they agreed.

Now, he was tied to a chair in the middle of some warehouse along the river. A foghorn blared in the distance.

*Shit, the wire,* he thought, wondering if they'd found it. Did they know he was ratting to the feds? His pulse quickened. The last thing he remembered was entering Vinnie's Lincoln Town Car.

Even though he lived the life of a mobster, he never thought he'd be in this position, betrayed by his employers and taken captive. People in his line of work always stayed in the present, only thinking of the future in terms of how much money they'd have stashed away when they finally retired.

Then the shit hit the fan and his world had been turned upside down. And for what? He still didn't know the reason for Vinnie's betrayal, but he'd show Vinnie by turning the tables on him. He would have loved to see the man's face when he found out who turned on him. The whole underworld, friend and foe, would be in shock that Michael had sung to the feds. And as he sat comfortably in his new home, with his new name, he would relish knowing how Vinnie was rotting away in prison. He felt bad for involving the old man, but that was the price for having an idiot son.

The witness protection program sounded good, not ideal, but better than his alternative. The minute he'd agreed to wear a wire, the feds were ready to scoop up his family and place them in protective custody. But Michael knew that wouldn't work. If his boss got wind that his family had vanished, the man would get suspicious of something. Michael would be a dead man.

Now, sitting tied to a chair, he knew his witness protection deal was most likely over.

He heard the echo of footsteps in the distance. People were approaching. He tensed, trying to prepare for what was to come, knowing death was most likely not far off.

"Nothing to say, you dirty rat?" Vinnie's voice said from the shadows.

"I'm not a rat," Michael said.

Vinnie, a hulking man with a protruding chin and sunken eyes, strolled into the light. Two of his goons—Johnny and Scottie—stood by his sides.

*Shit*, Michael thought, feeling his throat tighten. Johnny and Scottie were real lowlifes, men that liked to punish for sheer enjoyment. Vinnie only brought them around when he wanted to torture someone, to really put a hurt into a guy and keep his own hands clean.

Michael thought about saying the "safety" phrase, *It sure is hot in here*, but he had no idea if he was still wired. Once he said that, the feds would swarm the place, unless Vinnie had found the wire and tossed it. He prayed that wasn't the case, for that little device was his only hope at getting out alive.

First, he needed to get as much information on Vinnie as possible, fulfill his part of the deal with the feds. He'd already gotten some stuff at an early meeting, but nothing damning. Vinnie might be a wild killer, but he was always careful with his words.

Vinnie walked up to him, a toothpick sticking out of his mouth. The two goons circled behind Michael. He tried not to show his trepidation, but he stiffened, unable to help it. He knew the deal. The goons were a scare tactic. Not being able to see the men, not knowing what they were going to do and when they were going to do it, was frightening.

Vinnie pulled the toothpick from his mouth and flicked it at Michael's face. "You thought you could cut a deal?"

"Look, Vinnie, you know I'd never rat, so what's this about?"

Vinnie nodded, a grin spreading across his face. He rubbed his stubbly chin, looking as if he was thinking about something, then shot in and punched Michael in the gut.

Pain radiated throughout Michael's torso as the breath was forced from his lungs. He couldn't draw air back in, the psycho having hit his solar plexus.

"Hurts, don't it?" Vinnie asked.

When the ability to draw in a breath finally came back to him, Michael wheezed in a breath. "Please, Vinnie . . . Tell me what this is all about."

"No. I'm going to let my boys go to work on you. Make *you* tell me what you've been up to."

"I got busted. Set up. I don't know by who, but I'm not ratting. You know—"

Vinnie backhanded him, causing Michael and the chair to fall over.

"Damn it," Vinnie said. "See what you made me do? You got me so mad I lost my cool and hit you in your pretty face. I could've broken your jaw, and then what?"

Vinnie hit hard, but it was nothing Michael hadn't felt before. Feeling a trickle of blood dribble down his chin, he said, "What the fuck is this all about, man?"

Vinnie ordered his goons to pick Michael up.

"You see," Vinnie said, pacing back and forth within the circle of light. "This is why I brought you guys." Michael realized Vinnie was speaking to his men. "We're dealing with Michael Scofield. Hitman extraordinaire. Tough guy." Vinnie shook his head. "He won't crack easy, fellas." He stopped and stared past Michael and at his men. "So get to it."

"Wait," Michael said. "I've earned enough respect to have you tell me what's going on. Who's accusing me of being a rat?"

"We've got our sources. That's all a gun-for-hire like you needs to know."

Michael was starting to worry, but he kept his poker face on. This could all be a test, though he doubted it. "Did I rat on you when you killed that bodega owner over on 19th? Or when you killed Jimmy Tulips?"

Vinnie shook his head as if disappointed. "I should just shoot you in the head and be done with it like I promised my old man, but I love a good show, so fuck him." Vinnie stepped close and lowered his head to Michael's chest. "Yeah, I killed those men. Blew their fucking heads off."

Shit. Vinnie knew about the wire and he had most likely gotten rid of it. "It sure is hot in here," Michael said, regardless, hoping that somehow, he was still wearing the listening device.

Vinnie's eyebrows knitted together. "Huh?"

"I said, 'it sure is hot in here.'"

"I'm quite comfortable," Vinnie said. He glanced at his goons: "You guys warm?"

"No, boss," Scottie said.

"Not at all, boss," the other said.

"Is that some kind of code?" Vinnie asked. "You waiting for the cavalry, because they ain't coming." He pulled out the listening device that had previously been taped to Michael's groin. It was smashed, the plastic splintered.

"Tell me," Michael said, knowing he was going to die. "Why'd you set me up?"

"Because I don't like you."

"Bullshit. We never saw eye to eye, but that's not it. What happened? Is it about the lawyer, because I didn't talk?"

"Bullshit," Vinnie shouted. "You're a fucking liar and I'm going to enjoy watching you suffer."

"You're a coward, Vinnie. You can't even own up to the truth to a dead man."

"I ain't no coward. It was time for a change. The old man's time is up. He's sick. All he talks about is you. How upstanding you are. How I should be more like you. Well fuck that and fuck you." Vinnie came in and hit him across the face with a right. Michael's head jerked sideways, his neck cracking from the momentum. Pain shot into his head. He grunted as he straightened himself out, his neck barking. He dabbed at his stinging lips and tasted fresh blood.

"So this is all about your jealousy? Jealousy of a lowly hitman? A non-made man? An outsider for hire?"

"You ain't no outsider, asshole. You're as part of this family as . . ."

"Go ahead, say it," Michael said, egging the man on. There was no reason to be cautious with his words. He wasn't leaving the warehouse alive and they were the only weapon he had left to use against the man. Inflict as much mental pain and anger onto Vinnie before he met his maker. Vinnie said nothing, so Michael spoke up. "I'm as important to your father as you are. How's that feel?"

Vinnie smiled, which surprised Michael. No, scared him. He'd expected the man to hit him again, maybe have one of his goons beat on him or slice him up.

"You know, there's nothing I can do to you that will hurt as much as what I'm going to do to your family."

"You leave them out of this," Michael said, feeling as if he'd been stabbed in the heart. "I swear, if you touch them—"

"You'll what?" Vinnie said, cutting him off. The big man chuckled as he ran a hand over his head. In a mocking tone, he said, "I swear if you touch them—" Vinnie then shook his head and laughed. "Is that the most typical line used in situations like this, or what?"

"Sure is, boss," Scottie said.

Michael got control of himself. "You leave them out of this. I'll tell you whatever you want to know. They aren't a part of this, and you know it. We don't touch our families."

Michael heard movement from behind. There was muffled sobbing and the sound of multiple shoes scuffing against the cement. He knew the noise well, having shoved his victims forward to their graves as he pressed a gun to their heads. It was the walk of doom. Most people didn't have the nerve to fight, hoping somehow they'd survive.

Then it hit Michael and the breath came out of him. It wasn't possible, he thought. He quickly prayed it not to be true.

Then he saw them: his wife and kids. They had duct tape over their mouths and their hands were tied behind their backs. Johnny had the wife in his control and Scottie had the kids.

"Put them on their knees," Vinnie said.

"Don't do this," Michael begged.

His wife, Bernadette, and his kids, Tommy and Bobby, were crying, tears streaking down their faces. Bernadette was staring at him, her eyes filled with panic. Snot ran from her nostrils. She was trying to say something, but he couldn't understand her.

Michael fought against his bonds with all he had, but it was useless. The duct tape wrapped around his body and the chair held strong. "You fucking bastard!" he screamed. "This isn't right. This isn't right. You're going to die for this. I'll make sure you suffer."

Vinnie laughed, his arms cradling his large belly.

Michael's wife, Bernadette, was silently pleading for him to do something. His children were petrified, crying, faces glistening with tears. Scottie swatted Bobby, his youngest, when the boy wouldn't stop squirming. Michael stared at the man, who only laughed, then pulled out a knife and held it to the kid's throat. He felt a rage within him like he'd never known, as if hydrochloric acid coursed through his veins. He couldn't allow this to continue, to let Vinnie hurt them. If he got free, he wouldn't let these men live another second. They needed to die by his hands.

But through it all, he knew, deep down that there was nothing he could do. He was helpless and unable to protect his family.

"It's a good thing we taped their mouths shut, huh, boys?" Vinnie said.

"Yeah," Scottie said. "Whiny little shits."

"Let them go and I'll tell you everything I know," Michael said, trying to keep his cool. He needed to remain business-minded, like when he did a job. "I'll give you a head's up on what's coming. What the feds know."

Vinnie stepped in front of Bernadette and grabbed her by her jaw. "You've got yourself a real hottie here, Michael. I thought about doing her in front of you, one last screw before she leaves this world, but I already blew my load with this whore I'm seeing over on $5^{th}$."

Michael tensed every muscle in his body, holding back his need to scream and threaten. "Please, Vinnie," he said, seething. "The feds are going to tear your family apart if—"

Vinnie shoved Bernadette to the floor. She lay there for a few moments before Johnny reached down, grabbed her by the hair and yanked her back to her knees.

Michael ground his teeth, not sure how much longer he was going to be able to control himself. He took a long breath, reminding himself that his words needed to be chosen carefully, especially around a psycho like Vinnie. His wife and kids' lives depended on him.

"I see the anger on your face," Vinnie said, standing before him. "This could've all been avoided if you'd just gone away like you were supposed to."

"And I would've, if you hadn't set me up."

"Yeah, I'll admit it. It was me." The big man chuckled. "I mean, actually me who planted the gun. I didn't use some lackey. I wanted to make sure I was the one responsible for your downfall."

"All because your old man liked me?"

"You're a suck up. A piece of loyal shit. I mean, what kind of hitman is loyal? You're supposed to be cold, go to the highest bidder, right? But you'd never work for me. I was going to have you rot in prison for a few years before I had you killed, but then you made a deal." He shook his head. "I couldn't believe it. Michael Scofield going to the feds."

"I had no choice. You set me up. You broke the code first. I was only serving you what you deserved."

His kids continued to sob as the rain rattled against the roof. He wanted to let his children know they were going to be okay, but he had to stay on point.

"When Pop found out you ratted, he flipped out. Almost had a heart attack. His practically adopted son turned rat. Well, that couldn't stand. You needed to be made an example of. It was on his order that your family be rounded up and brought here."

"Bullshit," Michael said. "He'd never condone killing them."

"Okay, you're right. I lied. But since I'm going to be the one in charge soon, I'm starting a new policy. Fuck with me, your entire family dies."

Michael knew there was nothing worse than snitching. It was a guaranteed death sentence for the person, but never for the family, especially children. Mickey didn't know the truth. Didn't know his own son had started the ball rolling.

"I still can't believe you ratted us out," Vinnie said.

"I didn't. I only ratted you out. Got you on tape a number of times. You're finished."

"Yeah, right. If the feds had anything on me, I'd be locked up and you'd be safe. You didn't know we had people everywhere, including the police department? I mean, come on."

Michael knew some of the cops were on the Samson's payroll, but when the feds were involved, he decided to take a chance. Figured he'd be okay. Figured they'd be on top of things and make sure he was safe. He'd been very wrong.

Vinnie glanced at his Rolex. "It's getting late. I got to get up early and do some things."

"Vinnie, don't do this. Leave them alone. I got info you can use."

"Nah. This is something I've been waiting for, and for some time. Nothing gets to you. I've seen you in action. You're cold. Seeing you like this is . . . what's the word?

"Euphoric," Scottie said.

"Yeah. Euphoric."

"You're a fucking coward. You'll never be your old man. You're a fat loser who can't get it up. That's right, everyone knows about your problem, you piece of shit. I'll see you in hell."

Vinnie's face darkened. His mouth tightened into a thin line. Michael thought he was going to come at him, pound on him for a while, but then his face softened. "I want you to know true pain, and this is the best way I know how to give it to you."

Johnny slid the knife he'd been pressing against Bobby's neck into the sheath on his belt, then pulled a gun from his jacket and pressed the barrel against Bobby's head. The weapon had a silencer on it.

Bernadette muffle-screamed, her eyes bulging. She tried getting to her feet, to get to her son, but Scottie kneed her in the back and held her in place. She continued to struggle, which any loving mother would do, so he pulled his sidearm and walloped her in the back of the head. She went down, but was not out.

"Get her up," Vinnie said. "She needs to see this. See that her husband failed."

"Vinnie, don't do this," Michael said. "He's just a kid."

Vinnie nodded.

The gun in Johnny's hand jerked as it fired; the sound nothing more than a whisper.

Bobby's head disappeared, his lifeless body falling to the floor.

"Noooooooo!" Michael yelled.

Johnny executed Tommy next in the same fashion, sending the youngster's brains across the floor.

Everything slowed down. Nothing seemed real. His wife was throwing up, the vomit escaping from where the tape had come free, the silver adhesive dangling from one cheek.

Michael screamed and screamed. He stared at his dead sons, taking in the horror, letting it punish him. They were dead because of him, because of his failings.

"That's disgusting," Vinnie said, referring to Bernadette's vomiting. Her blouse was caked with the oatmeal-looking upchuck. He grabbed her from Scottie and dragged her over to Michael. Her eyes were glazed over. She wasn't all there anymore.

Vinnie released her. She continued to vomit, the sounds like a monster's roar. There was blood coming out now, as if her stomach lining was coming free. She started convulsing, her face turning red. She was choking. Michael fought to get free, to save her, but movement was impossible.

"She's dying, Mikey," Vinnie said. "Shitty way to go. Let me end it quickly for her." He pulled out his silver plated .45 and shot her in the head, the gunshot deafening. Her head exploded, the contents mixing on the floor with some of Tommy's. He shot her again and again, laughing. Her head was now a tangled mess of hair, pulpy gore and blood.

Michael sagged, dead inside.

Vinnie replaced the gun to his jacket. He held Michael's face up so he could look into his eyes. "This is all on you."

"Kill me. Just kill me," Michael said, no longer caring about vengeance. He just wanted to die and be with his wife and kids, as long as hell didn't claim him.

"You're not getting out that easy, asshole," Vinnie said, then clobbered him over the head, knocking him out cold.

# CHAPTER 2

Michael awoke some time later. His head ached with a throbbing that radiated down his spine. Other than that, physically, he felt fine. His mental state was something else, which was quickly coming apart at the memory of the warehouse.

The bright glow of a portable lantern illuminated the room he was in, revealing a multitude of oil drums that were stacked on top of each other to the ceiling and as far back as the light would allow him to see. The walls looked about ten feet tall. They weren't smooth, but squared off ridges that ran vertically. Smudges, scratches and nicks marked the walls as if numerous items had been going in and out of the place on a regular basis. Then, it dawned on him . . .

He was in a shipping container.

For a moment, he wondered if it had all been a dream, if his wife and kids were safe at home. Then he saw the coffins stacked against the far wall, the boxes rudimentary and cheaply constructed from plywood, like something out of the old west.

Michael's heart sank and his throat tightened.

He tried to stand, but was unable. His legs gave out and he fell to his knees. He cried out and screamed until his throat was hoarse. He sat back on his heels, wondering why he'd been left alive. It didn't make sense. Unless the old man, Mickey, wanted to see him before he killed him. But he wasn't tied up. Even unarmed,

14

Michael was a dangerous man. So, no, he doubted anyone was coming to pay him a visit.

He sat up, getting hold of himself. He needed to figure a way out of here. They'd left him alive, which was a terrible mistake on their part, for vengeance would be his.

His eyes fell to the coffins again. He didn't want to look at them, would have preferred if they were covered by a tarp, but he couldn't help it.

Getting to his feet, he dragged himself over to the boxes. The wood smelled fresh. He had no idea who was in which one. He leaned his head against the top coffin and cried. "I'm sorry. I'm so sorry. I . . ."

He pounded on the box, anger rearing its ugly head. "I'll kill them all. I promise." He almost felt ridiculous promising his dead loved ones that he'd get revenge. His kids were just that, kids. Their souls hadn't been touched by the wickedness of man. Vengeance and the need for it were foreign to them, and to his wife. She knew what he did, not the details, but she knew he was involved with illegal, mob-related activity. But things were different now. He was certain she'd want revenge for her sons.

He wondered if she'd hate him for bringing this on, but he told himself he hadn't. They both knew the life and what it involved, which weren't the families. The families were always untouched, even helped monetarily when the man of the house was killed. For that reason alone, he knew his wife would want him to live so that he could kill Vinnie and his goons, those wretched, evil scumbags.

He needed to feel hate, rage, to be furious. If he let the sadness in, he'd crumble. Now more than ever, he needed to be a killing machine of destruction and death. When it was over, he'd rest, maybe even die, but until his last breath, he would remain angry and mean.

He came away from the coffins and looked around, trying to come up with a way out, when the floor tilted. He stumbled before bracing himself against the wall. The container had swayed, as if it had been lifted. He wondered if he was being shipped somewhere. He went over to the door and tried opening it, but it didn't budge. He figured as much.

He banged on the walls, the pounding dull. With the container full, the echoing noise he hoped to make wasn't going to happen. The place was too packed with oil drums. He knocked on one, and by the sound it made, he could tell it was filled with something. Sniffing, he didn't detect an odor, save the musty smell of the container and the freshly cut wood of the coffins.

He stood completely still and closed his eyes. There was a slight swaying still present, and then he realized that he wasn't suspended somewhere, but he was on a ship at sea. Part of a barge, most likely, the container he was in stacked among hundreds of others.

The mystery was unfolding, though he still couldn't figure out why he'd been left alive. They knew how dangerous he was. The battery-operated lantern was left for him. They wanted him to know where he was, and to see the coffins. Was he being shipped to some developing country to be sold into slavery? Taken prisoner and tortured? And what was in the oil drums? It was clear that his punishment wasn't over.

He tried to open one of the barrels, but the lid appeared to have been welded on. He needed a place to hide, so he could surprise whoever came for him. It would most likely be more than one person. A small group, and they'd be armed, but he would hide nonetheless.

Michael shook his head, frustrated. There was nothing he could do except wait and see what happened. Unable to find a decent place to hide, he searched for something he could use as a weapon. Again, there was nothing available save the lantern and his fists.

He paced the small area allotted to him, then realized it would be best to save his strength, and sat against the doors. The swaying picked up a bit, as if rough waters were about.

As time wore on, he grew tired, and as hard as it was to imagine falling asleep, he did.

# CHAPTER 3

Michael was startled awake by a loud boom that shook the shipping container and rattled the oil drums. The highest coffin tumbled to the floor in a deafening crash and broke open. A tiny arm protruded from the wreckage. By the size of it, he knew it was his youngest, Bobby's. The breath was forced from his lungs as devastation racked his core like a sickness.

The container continued to shudder as if an earthquake were occurring. Michael braced himself against the wall as he got to his feet. With his mouth agape, he sucked in air, trying to calm his nerves and prepare for what was happening—of course, blind to the goings-on in the outside world.

He heard the mechanical sounds of hydraulics, and then another boom that rattled the container, as if something large had gripped it. He'd been on the docks in Brooklyn and Chicago, and he knew the sound of a crane clamping down onto a container. The container swayed and the sensation of being lifted fell over him. His legs grew heavy, like a rapidly rising elevator, and he knew the box had been hoisted into the air.

Then the momentum ceased, and he was thrown against a barrel as the container changed direction. Whoever was operating the crane had little regard for the container's contents. A quick glance over his shoulder and he saw that Bobby's body had slid out almost completely from the collapsed coffin. The dead flesh was as pale as a white bed sheet. The lips were dark blue, but that was all the identifiable parts. The upper portion of the head was a pulpy, skin-flapping mess.

Michael reeled, then bent over and vomited. A moment later, he stumbled to the floor and slid across it before slamming into a wall. He smashed his right knee, the pain sharp. He cried out, but he held onto the wall as the sensation of being lowered fell over him.

This was it, he thought. The moment of truth was upon him.

He remained positive, reminding himself that they had kept him alive, which meant there was the possibility of escape.

He heard a noise and looked up to see that narrow slats in the top of the container had slid open. Sunlight poked through, along with the salty smell of ocean air. "Hey," he yelled. "I'm in here. Help." He fought through his biting knee pain, and climbed atop one of the barrels to get closer to one of the narrow openings. There was no way he would fit through, but there was nothing to stop his voice from escaping.

"Hey, I'm in here. Help."

He continued to yell as loudly as he could, cupping his mouth to concentrate his voice through the opening. Then slats in the floor opened, each one about twelve inches long and two inches wide.

Michael climbed down and hurried over to one, the salty air wafting through. He saw rough seas below. White foam had formed at the top of small waves, no doubt caused by the water crashing against the ship's hull.

The container came to a jerking stop and he was forced to the floor. He pushed himself up and began yelling through one of the slats again, begging for help and trying to alert anyone who would listen that he was inside.

Something thudded behind him. He spun in that direction and saw a small package. Someone had dropped it through one of the slats. His stomach roiled. All his yelling was for nothing. Whoever was outside, knew he was here.

He hurried over to the package, which had fallen inches from his son's body. He pulled part of the coffin over it so he wouldn't have to look at it anymore, then picked up the package. It had weight to it and it was wrapped in thick, brown paper.

Tearing it open, he found an old cassette recorder, like the kind cops used to record interrogations before technology allowed them to wire the room. The words PLAY ME were written in black marker across the speaker grating.

Michael swallowed, his throat parched. He knew the message wasn't going to be something he wanted to hear, but figured it was going to answer his questions as to why he'd been left alive and where he was going.

He looked around again at the unmarked oil drums. At the coffins. At himself. He thought about where he was. Though he hoped the ship had docked somewhere, and his container was being unloaded to shore, he knew better. He didn't want the last voice he heard to be Vinnie's, but he needed to know what was on the tape.

He pressed play.

A few moments of tape-rolling hissing, then: *In case you haven't figured it out by now, you're on a ship at sea.* The voice was Vinnie's. *I left you alive, figuring you'd want more time with your dead loved ones. And people say I'm a cold-hearted prick.* Vinnie laughed. *Anyway, I wanted to kill you slowly, make you suffer. Cut you into little pieces and feed you to the piranhas in my fish tank, but I figured this was better. A more fitting way for you to go. You can say goodbye to your family, and then be with them forever.* There was a pause of silence, the only sound being the hiss of the recorder as the tape continued to play. Michael thought the message was over, and then he heard a woman's laughter. Vinnie cleared his throat. *So, just know that your body, along with your family members' bodies, will be resting comfortably at the bottom of the Atlantic Ocean, never to be disturbed or found by anyone. You'll simply have disappeared, leaving those fucking feds to scratch their heads. Your case will be filed away, and soon enough, you'll be a forgotten memory for all who knew you. Well, except for me. I'll think of you every time I take a piss off my yacht. Oh, and in case you're wondering what's in those barrels? They're filled with some nasty stuff. Some lab's secret concoction that went bad. Some kind of experimental crap that really made a mess out of their test subjects. So I wouldn't go opening one up. Got a pretty penny for taking the shit off their hands, too. I'm thinking of adding a special waste-removal service to the family business, as there are a lot of companies needing this sort of thing, from what I've learned. We do so well with regular garbage, might as well. Anyway, go fuck yourself and good riddance to you and your rat-fuck family.*

That was it. The tape continued to roll, but there was nothing.

In a burst of rage, Michael grabbed the recorder with both hands, held it over his head and threw it to the floor at his feet. A loud thud reverberated around the room as plastic fragments splintered in differing directions. Not satisfied with its partial destruction, he raised his foot and smashed the device until it was nothing but a jagged pile of rubble.

When he was finished, he was breathing heavily. The fight was not out of him, though. "Hey, whoever's up there, I'll pay you a million dollars if you let me out of here. A million, you hear me?"

No answer.

He kicked the smashed recorder, the pieces scattering everywhere. He yelled in frustration, and then kicked one of the barrels. He turned and punched the wall. It couldn't end like this. It wasn't right. He needed to kill Vinnie, make him and those goons of his pay. Shit, he wanted the whole family to pay for allowing this to happen to him.

Michael growled, then bellowed a roar, unable to control his rage. His face pulsed with blood, but there was nothing he could do, except wait for the inevitable—his *sleep with the fishes,* as the saying went.

Then his stomach felt like it rose into his chest, as the sensation of weightlessness hit, and he knew the container had been released.

A bone-rattling, eardrum-rupturing blast struck his body as the container came to a crashing halt. Michael crumpled to the floor with the impact. Pain exploded in his already bruised knees. Something in his wrist cracked, and electric-like agony shot up his forearm.

Michael cried out. The light-headed, world-going-dark phase of passing out hovered over him, but when the chilled ocean water washed over his flesh, his head quickly cleared.

He sat up and saw the container filling with water. The slats in the floor and ceiling had remained open. They had been left that way to allow the ocean water in and the container to sink; otherwise, it might float around, eventually being discovered.

He was going to drown to death.

He needed to block the slats, but with what?

His clothing wouldn't work. The water would eventually leak through, and there were too many openings. His only chance was to push the oil drums over the holes and hope that would do the trick.

Heading to the closest drum, he shoved it with all his might. The thing wouldn't move. He then repositioned himself so that he could use his legs to push off the stack of oil drums behind the one he wanted to move. Using his legs and entire body's weight, he pushed with all his strength. His face turned red with the effort, veins popping out across his forehead. He felt the drum tilt, then slam back down. He tried again and again, rocking back and forth before the barrel finally tipped over and fell onto its side. Relief at the small victory filled Michael with much needed hope. He rolled the barrel over one of the open slats. He needed three more barrels to cover the other holes. The water was already at his knees. He didn't think he was going to have time. Once enough water entered, the drums would come loose from their stacks, maybe even float, making covering the holes impossible.

As he prepared to shove another barrel free, he noticed how the water was turning a fluorescent purple. Staring in confusion, his eyes went to the barrel and he saw that the lid had cracked open, a purple liquid leaking out. A chemical-like odor filled the air, a mixture of alcohol and ammonia. His eyes watered and his throat burned.

Knowing he didn't want the stuff touching him, he sprang out of the water and onto one of the barrels. Vinnie hadn't been kidding when he said the stuff was toxic. He knew the family had engaged in a plethora of illegal activity, but dumping this kind of stuff just wasn't right. People got what they deserved, but the planet didn't deserve to suffer because people were assholes. Regardless, his situation just got much worse.

He blinked rapidly, trying to stem the tears that were blinding his vision. The fumes were unbearable. His skin itched and his lungs felt as if he'd inhaled flame, but he had to fight through it, deal with each catastrophe as it came. He still needed to stop the container from filling up with water. Stop himself from drowning.

Positioning himself, he attempted to push over another barrel. If he had to get into the water, then so be it. He'd deal with the chemical and what it did to him later. Then, as he worked to tip the barrel, his feet slipped, his hands flew free, and he plunged face-first into the rising frigid ocean waters.

Michael shut his eyes and closed his mouth, but not before some of the water entered both. He pushed himself up and spat as he got to his feet. He wiped the water from his face, expecting to feel his flesh sizzle, but there was no pain. In fact, he felt fine. It was the fumes that were bothering him, his eyes and lungs continuing to burn.

The water was coming into the container too fast, and was up to his waist now. He needed to stop the flow while it was still afloat. He could barely breathe, though, and wondered if his lung tissue was disintegrating. His eyes and throat felt like someone was rubbing sandpaper over them.

A wave of dizziness fell over him, and he stumbled back, falling ass-first into the water. This time, he received a mouthful of the purple-tinged liquid. His palate flooded with an awful taste, like spoiled seafood, rubber and alcohol all mixed together. He gagged and swallowed, his throat soothed momentarily from the burning sensation.

He tried to get up, but his legs had no strength in them. His flesh itched like crazy, as if every inch of his skin was covered in ants.

Determined, he grabbed hold of a barrel, got his legs under him and rose to his feet. The room was spinning. He felt nauseous and puked. The stream of vomit was a swirl of fluorescent purple and red, his blood. His insides were on fire, the pain incredible, as if he swallowed razor blades. He knew everything he was feeling was due to the toxic waste, and understood he didn't have long to live. There was no point in denying it. He wasn't going to make it.

Instead of panicking, he was angry. He was fuming with hate and pissed off that the bad guy had won. He wasn't getting out of this oversized coffin. He'd lost. Revenge would only come from beyond the grave, if such a notion existed.

Staring at his arms, he blinked hard, not knowing if what he was witnessing was real. The flesh was slipping off them, as if he'd been wrapped in bandages. It fell apart in strips from his hands and forearms. He opened his mouth to scream, but only a phlegm-filled gurgle escaped. He touched his scalp and it came away like a badly placed wig. He was melting.

He stared at his gelatinous-looking arm and flexed, the red and white-lined muscles thinning and widening like some alien creature. His flesh continued to itch with a ferocity he couldn't stand, while his insides burned, as if he'd consumed a tall glass of hydrochloric acid. He let loose a gurgle cry. Blood mixed with chunks of his esophagus spewed forth. His left eye popped, then his right. Blind, he staggered about, feeling pieces of himself fall away as he plunged into the icy water.

His last thought wasn't of his family, but of Vinnie and how badly he wanted to exact revenge.

# CHAPTER 4

The container filled with water and sank into the ocean. It fell quickly, going down, like a stone tossed in a lake. Michael's ruined flesh—for the cells were still alive due to the purple-colored chemical—bobbed around like algae. The crushing power of the ocean increased with each descending foot. The container was crumpled in places, as if pelted by invisible boulders. Cracks formed throughout. The walls bent inward, but only slightly as the pressure equalized due to the open slits. Incredibly enough, the barrels of toxic waste remained intact.

The corpses' insides ruptured throughout, the trapped air escaping with vicious abandon.

The toxic chemical that had leaked from the drum was heavier than the water and settled along the container's bottom like fog on a damp summer morning.

As time wore on and things stabilized, sea life began to investigate. First, a tiny fish came along and entered the structure, attracted by the glowing purple water. It swam in the fog, growing ravenously hungry, and then fed on Michael's remains.

The fish remained there for days, not wanting to leave the purple haze, or its food source. The corpse was a feast, and the more it consumed, the more it wanted, gorging itself like a gluttonous pig. It cells mutated and it grew rapidly. It took on a human-like form, sprouting arms and legs.

Soon, other sea life crept in. The altered fish-thing protected its lair and killed all that entered, devouring prey. Unbeknownst to the critter, the toxic waste was changing it into something new, a creature never before seen on the planet. It used everything it ate, taking the DNA and absorbing it into its own, rebuilding itself. Along with its purple flesh, arms and legs, it grew claws, sharp teeth, a tail and tentacles.

Throughout its changes, the human DNA remained its main source. Its brain was reconstituted to that of a human, of Michael's. Within two weeks, it had grown too large for the container and ripped through it, realizing it needed to feed on bigger and more powerful creatures of the sea.

Leaving its lair felt right, like a hatchling departing from its nest. It swam out in search of new foods, devouring lobsters, crabs, sharks, worms, octopus, squid, manta rays, whales and anything else that came across its path.

# CHAPTER 5

Mickey Samson, the overweight, hairpiece-wearing head of the Samson crime family, sat in the back of his limo as it cruised the streets of Brooklyn. He still couldn't believe it. Michael, a man he'd treated like a son, was a rat bastard. He had hoped Michael would stick around after he retired. Help to steer his son in the right direction. Vinnie wasn't the brightest and had a temper, but with the right people around him, Mickey had hope for his son.

Mickey shook his head for what seemed like the thousandth time since he learned that Michael had gone to the feds. It just didn't make any sense. And over a simple gun bust? That too didn't add up. Mickey knew Michael's routine, knew the hitman was thorough, careful. Always cleaned up after a job. The guy never kept the murder weapon. So why had he had it in his car so long after the job?

After finding out that Michael had made a deal with the feds, Mickey ordered Michael dead. He'd been so enraged and shocked. Thinking about it now, he realized he should've had the bastard brought before him—find out exactly what happened and why he felt the need to rat.

"What's the matter, boss?" Paulie asked, sitting across from him. Paulie had been with Mickey for ten years, always by his side. "You feeling okay? You don't look so good."

"I'm okay, Paulie," Mickey said, waving him off. "I guess I'm still in shock and extremely disappointed."

"I know, boss," Paulie said. "We're all in shock over Michael, the rat bastard."

"I wish I'd kept my cool, looked him in the eye and put a bullet into him myself."

Paulie nodded, and after a few moments of silence had passed, he said, "Don't let that piece of shit bother you, boss. He ain't worth it. No one that goes to the feds or the cops is worth a roach's turd. The snitch bitch is where he belongs—swimming with the fishes." Paulie laughed. "It never gets old saying that."

The only comfort Mickey got out of Michael's death was that there'd been no serious damage to him or the family, this news coming from a source he had in the F.B.I.

The authorities—the ones not on his payroll—were always after him, and this was just another example of how none of them would ever see him behind bars.

Mickey had gotten used to avoiding prison, so much so that he began to think he was untouchable. Of course, the cops coming after him was all part of the game, the business. But this latest affair . . . Well, that put a scare into him like never before. Men like Michael were supposed to have a code. No self-respecting gangster would ever think of squealing.

Mickey had been contemplating retiring for a while now. Michael's betrayal was just one more reason he knew he'd made the right decision. He'd been head of the family for over twenty years. The new generation was different, unreliable. Maybe Vinnie wasn't too hot-headed. Maybe he was exactly what the next line of criminal needed.

Mickey looked at Paulie.

"What is it, boss?"

"I've got something to tell you, Paulie. You've been with me for a long time, my friend, and I want you to hear it from—"

Mickey's words were cut short by a thunderous blast. A fraction of a second later, he flew from his seat and smashed into the door. The window shattered as his head collided against it. The interior of the limo resembled a dryer set to high speed. He and Paulie, along with glass shards, loose change, keys and bottles of liquor tumbled around as the car rolled over. He felt something snap in his right arm. Pain bloomed. Then his head collided with Paulie's knee and he was knocked out cold.

\*\*\*

Mickey came to. The acrid smell of urine filled his nose. His crotch was wet and warm. He'd pissed himself. His head was foggy. Pain engulfed his body, but his back and right arm hurt the most. He was afraid to open his eyes.

The sound of footsteps crunching against glass fragments startled him. Someone was approaching the wreck. He attempted to call out for help, but his voice was merely a whisper.

The creak and groan of metal sounded. Someone was opening the door.

Still, he kept his eyes shut.

"Paulie?" he said.

No answer.

Then he felt someone grab him and pull him free of the wreckage. He finally opened his eyes and saw the limo. The windows had been smashed out and the car looked like it had been hit by a train, the back end twisted and bent. Then he saw the large dump truck, the front end with a few dents and scratches, but nothing that would hinder the vehicle from doing its job.

He couldn't see who was holding him. The pain wracking his body was too much and he passed out again.

\*\*\*

Mickey woke up on a cold cement floor that was layered in dust and grime. Sunlight shone through a glass-less window about seven feet from the ground. He grimaced at the stale and musty odor. Glancing around, he saw dingy cinder block walls decorated with layers of graffiti. A rat squeaked somewhere in the distance.

Mickey looked around for Paulie, but found himself alone.

A tall figure entered the room through a door-less entrance. Mickey couldn't make out any features, the person a silhouette of darkness.

Even though pain enveloped him and his situation appeared dire, Mickey wasn't afraid of the individual. He was still alive, obviously taken as part of someone's plan. He'd only wished they'd stopped the car by some other means and taken him by gunpoint, avoiding injury. Some low-class morons, he thought.

He was the head of a major crime family. A man who had been shot and stabbed numerous times, and when he was younger, had made professional street fighters look like chumps.

"Do you know who I am?" he asked, through pained breaths.

"He's awake," the figure said.

Footsteps sounded, and then another person entered the room.

"You fellas have made a big mistake. I suggest you give me a phone and scram before I find out who you are. If that happens, you're as good as dead. You hear me?"

Neither figure said a word.

"Where's the guy that was with me in the back, Paulie?" Mickey asked. "You better not have—"

"He's dead, old man," the first figure said.

The breath caught in Mickey's chest. He loved Paulie like a younger brother. One who he looked out for and who looked out for him. Anger took over. He could no longer play the nice guy routine. "You guys are dead. There's no where you can hide. I'll find you if it's the last thing I do."

The silhouettes remained motionless.

Deciding he needed to play this differently, he lied—because anyone involved with his kidnapping was going to die—and said, "Look, I'm just pissed off. You got one of my guys killed, but I understand this is business. You obviously want me alive, so get on with your demands."

"Always the tough guy with words," the second man who entered the room said, and Mickey stiffened. He knew that voice, knew it like his own.

"Vinnie?" Mickey said.

The figure stepped into the light. "Pops," Vinnie said, smiling warmly, arms out wide as if ready to accept a hug.

Mickey felt as if his brain had seized up. He knew his son was crazy, but this? It took him a moment to get his speech back. "W— what the hell is this about, son?"

"Taking over."

"What? I don't understand. Are you crazy?"

Vinnie slowly shook his head as he paced the room in front of Mickey. He popped a toothpick between his lips and twiddled it around. Mickey wanted to scream at his son, but held his tongue, knowing he needed to play it cool, for now.

"You know, Pop," Vinnie said. "You've gotten weak. You're an old man. I'm only taking what's rightfully mine."

"Boy . . . you need to stop this."

Vinnie laughed. "You see, that's what I'm talking about, Pop. You sound like a woman. Soft. You're a pussy. Where's the yelling, threatening, mean son of a bitch?"

Mickey's insides felt like they were crumbling. His one and only son was a psycho. There would be no saving him now. He'd put a bullet into him himself if he got out of this alive. Vinnie had simply gone too far.

"Vincent, you really screwed up. I was planning on stepping down. You know that. Was going to tell you, along with the others, tonight, when we met up. There was no need for this."

Vinnie's face went rigid. His eyes bore in on Mickey's, then he looked back at the figure still in shadow. Mickey guessed the guy was being cautious, not wanting to show his face should things go badly.

"I think he's telling the truth," Vinnie said to the man.

"Of course I am," Mickey said, fighting back a sharp stabbing pain in his right side. "You're next to lead. I've always known it."

"Bullshit," Vinnie roared, looking at Mickey again. "You treat me like a goon. Like one of your errand boys. You were never putting me in charge of anything but grunt work."

"Those things were only to make you stronger, give you the other side of the business."

Vinnie stepped up to Mickey, his hands balling into fists, knuckles cracking.

"Son, I know you're angry, but it's all going to be okay. Give me a week to alert the crew, then the family's yours."

"Too late, asshole," Vinnie said, backing up a step and smiling. "Everything's in motion. Your time is up. You should've put me in charge earlier, years ago. I earned it."

Mickey's eyebrows shot up. "What do you mean, 'everything's in motion?' What have you done?"

"I'm glad you asked," Vinnie said, then rattled off a bunch of names—all of Mickey's most trusted soldiers and bosses. "They're all dead, thanks to the meeting you had set up. The one you were heading to. The whole building blew, can you believe it?"

The color drained from Mickey's face. His body felt like it weighed a ton. He shook his head, his jowls wiggling. "No. No. Tell me you didn't, Vinnie."

"It's done."

"I don't believe you. Not even you're that stupid."

"I don't care what you believe. I can hear it in your voice that you know I'm telling the truth. You're scared."

"You need to be put down. You're dead. You hear me. Dead."

"I'm going to turn this family into what it needs to be. All that peace you'd brokered with the other families, those low-life gangs . . . all gone. I'm waging war, taking over the city. The numerous Samson family members' deaths will go down as a Matrone family hit. Rumors are being spread as we talk. That ought to start things heating up nicely. From there, alliances will splinter and all out war will follow."

Mickey had worked so hard to bring peace to the city. Everyone was, for the most part, satisfied with their territory, and making money.

"Why would you want this?" Mickey asked. "Everything was in balance. You had everything you could've wanted. The cops aren't going to stand for this. You'll bring heat like we've never seen, you stupid moron."

Mickey needed to wake from this nightmare. This couldn't be real, or be happening, but no matter how hard he tried to wake, he didn't, because he wasn't dreaming.

Then he remembered.

Michael Scofield.

His eyes grew wide. He glared at Vinnie. "It was you."

"Me?"

"You. You set up Michael. He was the first one of my men to go, wasn't he?"

Vinnie clapped his hands in mock congratulation. "Very good, you figured it out. I was going to make sure you knew before you died, but good for you."

"You're a disgrace."

"I did you a favor with Michael," Vinnie said, anger in his voice. "The guy ratted on his own. I had nothing to do with that."

"Yeah, after he found out what you did. After you set him up. He was only going after you for what you did to him. I applaud him for that." Mickey would never condone ratting under any circumstances, whether he was set up or not. Michael deserved to die for going to the feds, but Mickey had to pretend it was okay, simply to piss off his son.

Vinnie stared at Mickey, his face scrunched into a grimace. He looked ready to explode. "Okay to rat?" Vinnie turned, went over to the shadows and picked something up. When he came back into the lighted part of the room, he was holding an AK-47 assault rifle. "How does it feel to know you've lost everything, and had it all taken away by your goon of a son?"

Mickey coughed up a wad of phlegm and spit. "I'll see you in hell, boy."

Vinnie pulled the machine gun's trigger. The gun roared. Fire spewed from the end of the barrel. The room lit up like a disco. Bullets ripped into Mickey, shredding his flesh. The first few that entered his chest hurt quite a bit, but then his heart took one and exploded, leaving him numb. A moment later, a bullet pierced his skull and Mickey Samson was no more.

# CHAPTER 6

Jim Montrose leaned on the cruise ship's railing as he looked out over the vast ocean and the clear blue sky above. The constant gust of wind was refreshing and seemed to bring with it new life into his body and mind. He'd needed a change from Brooklyn, with its stale air, horn-honking, siren-ridden streets and garbage cluttered sidewalks. It was simply good to get away, to escape.

Life had been great for a while, but then it took a nasty turn a few years ago, after the death of William, his youngest son. His divorce was finalized a year later, and he'd been working—driving a cab—seventy and eighty hour weeks since.

Diving into work had been his only choice, a distraction, hence the reason for the long hours. But he also wanted to make sure his other son, Daniel, would never go without money if anything ever happened to him, including having money for college.

He loved Daniel and would do anything he could for the boy. There was no way he was going to allow his son to take out school loans and amass a debt that would swallow half of Daniel's paycheck when he got a job. Jim had too many friends with decent paying jobs that were in debt because of their college loans.

Jim's custody agreement allowed him to have Daniel on weekends and every other holiday. It had been complete and utter hell losing a son, and now he was losing time with Daniel, the weekends always flying by quickly. He wanted to move back in with his wife and be a family again, but he knew that was never going to happen.

Jim was still damaged, his psyche simply not right. He couldn't concentrate on simple tasks or sit alone in his apartment without the radio or television on. If there was silence, nothing for his mind to concentrate on, his thoughts went to his dead son. He loved remembering him, but sometimes it just hurt too much.

Not nearly as painful, but adding to his misery, was his knowing how much his wife despised him. He'd loved—still loved—Rebecca with all his heart. They'd been high school sweethearts. Rebecca was Jim's main girl, but he'd had flings on the side.

However, it was Daniel who he hated being apart from even more. Every Sunday night, when he had to drop him off at his mother's house, it felt like a piece of his soul was being torn from him. It wasn't fair. But then again, nothing in life was.

The death of William had been *the* downward turning point of his life; the reason things would never be the same, why he'd never look at anything with a truly warm heart again.

Jim had been at the park with his two boys when the unthinkable occurred. Instead of keeping an eye on them, he'd been flirting with a young woman, and didn't see the man abduct William.

Jim had always been a playboy. Sure, he loved Rebecca, but he loved women too. It was only right before his father passed away that he decided to focus more on being a family man. "My biggest and only regret, son," the man said, "was not staying faithful to your mother. She was a great woman who I didn't fully appreciate until I lost her. I still had you and your brother, but our family was broken. Don't let that happen to you."

Jim hadn't been ready for a family, and he might never have been, but he dove in, regardless, figuring things would work out. He loved Rebecca, but he never fully appreciated her like she deserved. When he did finally realize what he'd lost in her, it was too late.

During his marriage, there had been too many willing and able women, and wearing his wedding ring only seemed to attract more, the naughty ones, the ones who loved to rock his world.

It was sad that it took his son being kidnapped to wake him up, to bring him closer to his wife, to learn to know what love is—if only for a short while. She'd caught him cheating twice before and forgave him, but after their son had been found dead, she could no longer love him, nor look at him. He had been the one looking after the kids. Letting her down was one thing, but letting their sons down was another.

The man who kidnapped William had been captured on video doing so, but by the time the authorities found him, William was dead.

The funeral was closed-casket.

During the divorce proceedings, Rebecca had gone for full custody, saying how Jim was an unfit parent and couldn't be trusted. In the end, the court didn't see the kidnapping as Jim's fault. There was no legal reason to deny him access to Daniel, so he received shared custody, just the shorter side of it. He didn't want the divorce to begin with. Didn't want to be apart from his wife and son. Nevertheless, in the end, he was grateful for what he received, because he wasn't going to be able to deal with losing another son.

During the divorce, he'd hit the bottle pretty hard and kept up the drinking whenever he was home and didn't have his son with him. He was able to control his drinking like that for a while, but knew it would eventually catch up to him. He hated being alone in his apartment, the quiet too much to bear. The pain of his son's voice echoing in his head was agonizing. There were times he swore he heard William's voice, his laughter, and felt as if he was being haunted.

It was only when he was working or when Daniel was over, that things seemed normal. He continued to drink, the activity getting more frequent until he needed the alcohol even when Daniel visited. He was managing. No one was getting hurt, so he kept self-medicating. Why change something that worked, he thought. Then one day, he got too drunk when his son was over and didn't wake up even when Daniel tugged at his arm. The boy wound up calling his mother, who called the police. When the cops arrived, followed soon after by Rebecca, Jim explained that he simply wasn't feeling good and that his son was fine. Rebecca went to court and tried to get full custody, but the whole thing proved to be a misunderstanding in the court's eyes and custody remained the same.

However, the possibility of losing his only remaining son really hit him hard. He sought counseling to help him deal— something he'd fought, having not believed in it—and after a few months, he found himself feeling better than he'd had in a long time. Confronting his emotions, his past, the death of his son and how it wasn't directly his fault—but that he was partially responsible— all seemed to come together. He was able to ditch the alcohol completely and even joined Alcoholics Anonymous.

Having gotten used to working long hours and making a lot more money, he kept up the schedule, for his son's future and for himself. He didn't have many friends and most of them looked at him as either a poor soul, damaged, or a bad parent. He preferred to be in his cab, talking with people who didn't know him, didn't judge him or give him looks of distain or sadness.

It took some time, but he'd finally decided he had suffered enough and needed a break from everyday life. He booked a European cruise. The ship departed from Manhattan and would make stops in England, Ireland, France and Spain, before returning to the city.

Now, staring out over the world, the horizon seeming like some never-ending plain, he realized how grand life was. Physically, he was merely a speck in it. If he disappeared, the world would go on as if nothing had happened. It was funny how he used to think he was the center of the universe and that what he experienced was earth shattering. But it wasn't, it was individual shattering. As tiny as people were when compared to the planet's vastness, he found it amazing how much more vast the human mind could be. There was so much to look forward to in the world. So much peace if a person allowed it in. Most of an individual's trouble was of *their* own doing, and if managed properly, the problems could be fixed or dealt with, even for someone like Jim.

Something tickled his left ankle. He glanced down and yanked his foot back, then stumbled into a wall. He couldn't believe what he was seeing. There was a purple tentacle—seemingly glowing— on the deck. The underside of the thing was lighter in color than

36

the top. At first, he thought an octopus had somehow crawled up the side of the ship, but when he stepped forward and peered over the railing, he saw that the tentacle was coming from the water below—the thing snaked up the side of the cruise liner like a vine of ivy.

Jim stepped back, keeping his eyes glued to the thing. The tentacle was inching about, as if prodding the ship, testing the surroundings. He looked left and right, but there was no one around. The closest people were up front and not looking in his direction.

He stared in wonderment, feeling his ankle begin to burn. Glancing at it, he saw that the flesh was smoking, the skin red and blistering. *What the hell?!*

Then the suckers along the tentacle opened and extended outward, like carnivorous blossoming flowers growing out of some tropical plant. Tiny mouths lined with pointy teeth nipped at the air.

Jim backed into the wall again, thudding his head hard. He didn't understand why he'd waited so long to do something. It was obvious the tentacle was dangerous and not something to play around with. He rubbed his head and made to run, when the thing shot forward and wrapped around his ankle. He cried out as it snaked with lightning speed up his leg. It ripped through his shorts as if they were made of tissue paper. The pain was white hot. Blood poured down his leg and he felt the thing's teeth gnawing at him. The tentacle wrapped around his testicles, and then slid up to his waist. He screamed for help and tried to break free, but the tentacle was too strong, like steel wrapped in hardened gel. He reached down to pry it off, but the sucker mouths bit into him and took three of his fingers.

Before he knew it, he was lifted off the deck and slammed into the wall of the ship. The tentacle was around his chest now, and a moment later, it was around his head, wrapping him up like a mummy. His flesh was on fire as the small but deadly mouths chomped away at him. They were eating him down to the bone like hungry piranhas. The tentacle continued to squeeze tighter as he writhed in agony, unable to scream when his voice box was taken. He knew death was imminent and only wished it would come quicker.

# CHAPTER 7

Though the prey was small, almost insignificant, the creature enjoyed its latest meal. It had seen the cruise ship from a great distance. The object was rather large when compared to other sea life, and it remained at the surface, like a dead whale, yet it was moving. The creature knew it wasn't a living or dead thing, but it had sensed life among it. No, it had sensed multiple lives, like a school of fish. Curious, the creature swam to it, keeping low in the depths. It then sent a tentacle to explore, finding the smooth sides of the object rather dull and unappealing, until it found life on the thing.

The meal was coursing through its vessels now, pieces of flesh being brought to various parts of its body and added to it. The creature absorbed everything it ate, taking the parts it wanted, the parts that would benefit it, the parts that would make it stronger.

The human it had consumed knew pain, true and terrifying pain. The worst kind. It had lost a loved one.

*Love?* It knew the word, but didn't understand it, not fully. The creature's brain was still developing, sifting through its former human mind.

Waves of emotional angst circulated within the creature, triggering its own past-anguish over something similar. It was unlike anything the creature or its parts had felt, except for the human that constituted its ability to think. Its name had been Michael.

The creature bellowed a wail, sending sonic waves throughout the waters. Unlike physical pain, this new, yet old, sting was worse. It threatened to bring the creature down, stop it from existing.

The human, the Michael, was a part of it, the part that allowed it to think and act without relying on instinct.

*Loss. . .*

It remembered the feeling of it. Of failure. Like being stabbed and gutted, having its insides yanked out. There was a sadness so deep, so debilitating that it couldn't quite fathom it now. Unable to deal with these emotions, it cried out as if struck. It shook with fury and confusion. It wanted to tear at its chest and remove the terribleness it felt inside.

It wasn't whole, it remembered. Something had been taken from it. A piece of its . . . soul?

Humans had souls, it remembered, and it being part human, wondered if it still had a soul.

Fragments of memories came roaring back.

A loved one.

No. Loved *ones*.

It had a family. A wife—*wife?* A son. No, it had sons. *Sons?*

Its mind worked feverishly to translate these things, and it came up with new words it could understand: offspring and mate.

It didn't understand how this could have been. It was a sea creature, a monster of the deep that prowled, killed and swam.

But it was partially human, it knew, and it was this human part that was the problem. Allowed it to act differently than its sea brethren. Made it feel different, like it didn't fully belong.

At its size and strength, its fear of predators was nil, save for one—man. The human part of it, the Michael part of it, had had an enemy. Its human death had been . . . personal. Its sea brethren did not have such things. Animals were bound by nature's laws, the food chain. Mankind was an anomaly. A destructive and unnatural force. A cancer to the planet. Humans had hurt its animal family. They pursued sea life—sharks and whales for sport, for oils and decorations. They corrupted natural elements and created pollution, which was harmful for the ocean's ecosystem. They were responsible for killing fish, crabs, lobsters and other life without meaning to do so, but knowing and not caring. They hunted these creatures in droves as well, tearing apart the natural order of things.

Confusion and sadness overwhelmed it.

A burning sensation grew within its gut, and it knew this to be hate. The ball of heat grew and the creature's sadness turned to rage.

Flashes of a human flickered across its mind.

Vinnie . . .

Brooklyn . . .

What did this mean, it wondered.

The creature's anger flourished to new heights. It didn't understand why its rage increased when thinking of this Vinnie, but then it did know. The individual was responsible for the pain it was experiencing.

More flashes, this time of other humans. Female. Young ones. Dying, death, and agony. Wrongness.

Vinnie had been the cause.

The creature bellowed a roar.

It needed to kill the enemy, the humans, especially the one called Vinnie. It knew where to find him, but first, it needed to protect itself. Keep its identity a secret. It had to eliminate the humans on the ship before they had a chance to . . . to what?

To alert other humans. Somehow, the beast knew they could communicate over great distances. They would send others to hunt it down. The behemoth could not allow that to happen.

Rage engulfed the creature as it eyed the ship above. With a kick of its powerful legs, its webbed feet scooped up ocean water and propelled it toward the surface.

# CHAPTER 8

Timmy was on the balcony of his parent's cabin aboard the cruise liner when he saw the water bubbling just off the starboard bow. He wondered if a whale was about to surface, when a moment later, he saw a huge dome-shaped object topped with pointy fins emerge from the water. He stared opened mouth and wide-eyed at the spectacle. The thing kept rising out of the sea, its features becoming more visible as hundreds of gallons of salt water cascaded off it. He'd seen pictures of whales in books and on television, but never in real life, and never with spiny fins and with an actual face. Its eyes were dark voids hidden deep within its bony skull. The color was odd too—a fluorescent purple, like the glow stick he'd gotten at the circus last year.

His theory of it being a whale ended when the tentacles came out of the water. Fear struck his heart at realizing he was looking at a giant octopus, like the one from the movie he saw, where the giant octopus—or was it a squid?—attacked a ship.

The tentacles—like in the movie—shot forward and latched onto parts of the ship, one going right over Timmy's head to the cabin above. He heard a scream. The tentacle retreated, taking a naked woman with it. Timmy thought the creature was going to toss the woman into its mouth, but instead, she was tossed into the pulsating starfish-shaped orifice on the creature's chest. He thought he saw snake-like things slithering around inside, but he couldn't be sure. The tentacle came back toward the ship again, the

41

tip disappearing as it entered a doorway two cabins over. The cruise liner swayed and Timmy had to grab onto the railing to keep from falling.

"What the hell was that?" he heard his mother yell from somewhere in the room.

Timmy wanted to tell her it was a giant sea monster. He knew she'd never believe him, but he said it anyway, "Mom, come quick. It's some kind of giant monster."

"We must've hit a wave or come across some rough seas," his father said.

His mother groaned. "Get inside now, Timmy."

Timmy thought about doing as his mother asked, but he was too enamored at seeing a real-life monster, and hadn't even noticed that he'd wet himself.

The creature rose farther out of the water and towered over the ship, leaving the vessel shrouded in shadow. It had muscled arms and lobster-like armor across its body, segmented like the lobster itself, leaving partially exposed fleshy skin.

The creature roared with the sound like a continuous clap of thunder. The ship vibrated from the sonic waves. Glass windows along the vessel shattered. Timmy covered his ears, but it made no difference. When the bellow ceased, the air was filled with the static-like rush of thousands of gallons of water, as rivulets of the salty sea fell from its body.

The behemoth continued to ascend, finally stopping as its torso breached the surface. The sun was blotted out and the ship was cast into shadow.

Timmy was no longer captivated. He was frightened. His bowels released themselves and he no longer wanted to see the monster. He wanted it gone. He knew he should run into the safety of the cabin, but he was frozen in place, his fingers gripping the railing as if glued to it.

Then something from behind wrapped itself around him, and he screamed. The monster had grabbed him. He opened his mouth to scream again for help and heard his mother's frantic voice. "Timmy, it's me." He felt her warmth and her breath fall over him like the best security blanket a kid could ask for. He felt safe for a moment, and then his mother cried out in sheer terror.

From the corner of his eye, Timmy saw his father emerge from the cabin. He was looking up, his mouth agape, eyes bulging.

The creature was gargantuan, a true behemoth. With a single blow, Timmy knew it could destroy the ship, the cruise liner like a bath toy to it. He shivered as his mother held him tightly.

The creature's exterior glowed in various places, as if electric current were coursing through it. People were being pulled from the ship by the tentacles and tossed into the starfish-shaped orifice on its chest. One of the slits opened wide, and this time, Timmy did see things slithering around inside. He shook with fright and wondered why he and his parents weren't hiding somewhere inside the ship. Maybe they knew something he didn't, he thought, like how—according to some movies—not all monsters were evil. Some were simply misunderstood and confused. Maybe the creature was only eating the bad people, thinning the world of its evildoers.

The monster's neck was hillside-thick and rose into its head like the trunk of a giant sequoia. Its shoulders resembled a gear-donning football player's. It had a powerful-looking jaw that took up half its head and angular teeth that appeared sharp enough to pierce through the toughest steel ever made.

It opened its mouth and roared again, but this time, an eel-like tongue shot out. It whipped at the air and hissed angrily. The behemoth came closer, allowing the eel-tongue to reach the ship. It smashed into the front end, tore a chunk away, then slithered inside the hull. A moment later, it retreated back into the monster's mouth with passengers' arms and legs protruding from its maw.

The behemoth's chest, sides and back were teaming with octopus and squid-like tentacles. The appendages seemed infinite as they continued to retrieve people from the ship, while others simply flailed about wildly. Timmy thought he'd seen all it had to offer, things his nightmares would plague him with for years, should he live past this day, but then its tail rose from the depths. The thing was lined with spikes, like puffer fish quills, and a giant-sized lobster claw sat at its end.

Winged serpents came from the starfish orifice in droves and slithered across the behemoth's body, adding what seemed like an extra living skin. Some took flight for a second, fluttering in the air before reattaching themselves to the creature again.

The creature roared once more and the ship rocked as the tentacles strained. Timmy's mother screamed along with his father. A chorus of other frightened calls echoed around the ship. Then the twisting and crunching of metal filled the air, overpowering all other sounds.

The cruise liner tilted at a steep angle. Timmy's dad hadn't been holding onto anything and went flying over the railing. Timmy's mother cried out, her voice the loudest Timmy had ever heard it. She fruitlessly reached over the railing, but her husband was already gone, rocketing toward the ocean and screaming the entire way. Then, just before he hit the water, a tentacle snatched him out of the air. The force must've been too much, because his dad's body was cut in half. Blood gushed. Timmy's dad's upper body was quickly entangled again by the tentacle. The man's waist and legs splashed into the water, but a moment later, the large chunk of meat was snatched up by another tentacle. Both pieces were brought to the creature's torso area, where the slithering winged serpents tore at the meat.

Timmy wanted to scream and wake himself from the nightmare, but his mother was hysterical, squeezing him so hard he couldn't breathe.

The ship was hefted into the air. More tentacles shot from the beast and into the ship, snaking through the hallways and pulling victims free. People with gashes across their bodies, some missing arms or legs, left trails of crimson behind as they were pulled from the ship. Screams continued to fill the air as they were either fed to the serpents or tossed into the starfish-shaped cavity.

A tentacle came at Timmy's head, but he managed to duck out of its way. He felt a warm, heavy liquid envelop him. His mother's hold on him loosened. He spun around and saw her headless body. Blood spurted from the stump like a fountain, sprinkling the deck area and Timmy in glistening red. His mother's head was impaled at the end of the tentacle, her lifeless eyes staring up at the sky. Tiny mouths along the appendage moved in rapid fashion as the tentacle wrapped around the head. A moment later, it was gone. The flesh, bone and hair had practically melted away as if his mother was a piece of cotton candy. Then her entire body was coiled within the purple, mouth-ridden tentacle and yanked off the ship, where it vanished into the creature's chest via the starfish orifice.

Drenched in blood and in shock, there was only one thing left for Timmy to do. He needed to hope he was having a nightmare. He knew every time he fell in a dream, he woke up, so he climbed onto the railing and jumped. He saw others around him tumbling from the ship and he wondered if they had thought the same thing. Maybe they were all dreaming.

The water approached fast. Timmy saw a number of people splashing around, trying to swim away. Blood had turned the sea red. Tentacles came from above and below, yanking people up and pulling them under. He closed his eyes, waiting to wake up. He'd sit up in bed, his heart pounding, kick off the covers and run to his parent's bedroom.

But the nightmare was real, and a moment later, he felt something smash into him, and then he knew no more.

# CHAPTER 9

The creature kept eating, not because it was hungry, but because it wanted to grow. It was going to need to be able to quell the threat that would be coming for it: the humans. It would do battle with them. By nature, they were warring creatures. They made weapons that could kill both small and large beasts, weapons that could wipe out all life on the planet.

They would certainly try to kill the behemoth, but it would not allow that to happen. It had a goal it needed to see come to fruition. Its wrath for vengeance was too great, as well as the anguish it felt for its dead loved ones. The humans were like a disease on the planet, had wiped out some of its sea brethren and had hunted other sea life to the brink of extinction.

Anger coursed through the creature. Its ability to think left it as rage took over and its primal instincts came to the forefront. The need to kill and to cause destruction was great. It still knew it needed to focus, for brash actions could result in its demise. It understood this on some level. It had a mixture of needing to fulfill its need for vengeance, but also the simple need to lash out at any and all humans.

For now, it decided to simply let its emotions take control.

It hefted the cruise ship in the air as its tentacles searched and found food. It sensed the dread of its prey, the humans no different from any other food supply on the planet. When a creature's life was in peril, it reacted and had the same feelings as anything or anyone else, human or beast.

A part of the behemoth enjoyed watching the small egocentric humans suffer. It felt great pleasure in knowing that the passengers, for that's what they were, it remembered, were tormented, aware that death awaited them and that they were scared *shitless*—as it knew the term to be.

The behemoth felt something within itself, some inner sensation it hadn't experienced yet in its current form. The emotion was a human one: humor.

It chuckled within itself. Laughter, it remembered, was a good thing. It was the opposite of anger. But this kind of laughter wasn't due to true happiness but to wickedness, because true laughter and joy didn't go along with hate and anger. The behemoth couldn't allow any kind of joy into its existence. Such a thing could kill its desire for revenge, causing the creature to lose its edge. It needed its fury to go on, and it needed to remain undeterred in its mission.

Michael's homeland, *New York City*, was a great place, strong and powerful. If the city crumbled, then the rest of the world would too. The creature wasn't sure how it knew this, but it did.

America . . .

There were other places, strong places that could pose a great threat to the creature. It would need to strike hard and fast, kill, devastate, then move onto these other places.

An image of the Vinnie human flashed across its mind, causing its anger to soar again. It growled, knowing of all the tiny and insignificant humans on the planet that this one in particular needed to die. Vinnie had wronged the creature, the human part of it when it had been mortal. This mattered, because without its human part, the Michael part, it wouldn't last long. It would not be cunning enough to know where to go, or how to outwit and overpower the humans that would surely attack it.

Thinking, it heard the word Brooklyn and knew that was where it needed to go.

The ship exploded in the creature's grasp. Pain erupted at the ends of a number of its tentacles, the appendages shredded and blown apart.

Reacting like an animal might, it released the vessel and let it crash into the sea. The fire that had engulfed the ship was extinguished. The water would protect the behemoth from man. Fire was man's ally, it remembered.

Its tentacles were strong, but easily hurt, so instead, it reached out with its hands and stopped the ship from sinking to the bottom, and then hefted it out of the water. The craft was partially bent in the middle, the hull breached, but still in one piece. The creature then sent its tentacles into the water and snatched up any humans—dead or alive—that had escaped from the ship.

However, there were still people in the ship as well. They would soon be dead, most of them already so. The creature was tired of the situation, and it needed to leave the area, for it knew that more people would come. The ship had most likely alerted other humans, humans with weapons. The creature was going to be hunted now. It wasn't afraid, not at its size and not while it was in the ocean. It was the predator, no matter if the humans came after it. It needed to be a cunning and wise predator though, and not allow its animal instincts to take over completely.

It twisted the ship in its grasp until the vessel was in two pieces, the steel hull splintering and ripped easily, as if the vessel were made of tin foil. More bodies spilled out, some bloodied, others charred, or alive and screaming.

The behemoth brought the ship to its facial mouth and opened wide. The serpent-tongue hissed, but remained within the maw. The creature then chomped down on the cruise liner, its powerful jaws and huge teeth crumpling the steel and glass with ease. In moments, the entire ship was gone, the gnarled pieces having slid down the creature's throat and into its acid-filled stomach. It would absorb the organic tissue of its meal, use what it needed, and then it would discard the rest at the bottom of the ocean, leaving nothing for the humans to find.

# CHAPTER 10

*The USS Gauntlet, a U.S. Navy aircraft carrier, is heading across the Atlantic Ocean on its way to Europe, where it will conduct readiness drills with a number of allied countries.*

"Sir, I'm receiving a rerouted distress call from one of our Coast Guard units stationed off the coast of Maine," said communications officer Daniels.

"Let's hear it," Lieutenant Commander Karnes said.

"This is North-Atlantic Ocean Lines ship 3204 out of New York City. We're under attack. I repeat, under attack. There's some kind of giant creature." Screams, yells, and curses could be heard in the background. "This is not a joke. I repeat. We're under attack. Please send help—" The message ended with screams, before it cut out to static.

The lieutenant commander's eyebrows came together. "Have you verified this, Daniels? Is this some kind of joke?"

"No, sir. It appears authentic."

The lieutenant commander shook his head. "See if you can raise the ocean liner on the comms."

The communications officer attempted to call the ship, but there was no answer.

"Are they within radar distance?"

"Close to thirty miles south of our position, sir. We're the closest ship to them."

"Set a course for their location. In the meantime, send up two Hornets. I want to make sure we aren't heading into a shit storm unprepared. And if this is some kind of prank, so help the bastard behind it."

\*\*\*

Tyrone Banks and Jeremy Stoddard got the call. The two men had been wingmen for years, and had been hanging out in the mess hall when they got their orders. Truth be told, neither man had been mentally ready for battle, not in the way they would've had they been heading to war. True, they were battle-tested and had been in the shit before, but this whole mission was supposed to be a piece of cake—a goodwill tour with allied nations, first stop the United Kingdom.

Suited up, each man climbed the ladder of their F/A-18 Hornet—the U.S. Navy's most common fighter jet. The fighter planes were armed with missiles, bombs and a Gatling-style rotary cannon called the M61 Vulcan that fired 20mm rounds at a high rate of speed.

The plane was quickly taxied into place and set up in the catapult—a giant slingshot designed to get the almost 37,000 pound craft into the air in two to four seconds. Banks gave the thumbs up and was in the air moments later with Stoddard right behind.

They flew side by side.

"So what's this about, some kind of sea monster?" Stoddard asked.

Banks laughed. "Yeah, we're going after Godzilla, didn't you know?"

"I always liked the good Godzilla better than the bad one. In this case, I hope it's the bad one so we can blow it away."

"Ok, ladies," Karnes said. "Stay sharp and ready. We really don't have any idea what we're dealing with."

"We'll keep a look out for Mothra too. We wouldn't want to get surprised from above," Stoddard said, chuckling.

Banks chuckled. The lieutenant commander groaned.

"Mothra's on our side, boss, don't worry," Banks said, laughing.

A few minutes later, they came upon where the cruise ship's last known location had been. Using the camera feeds from the aircraft, they saw nothing but water. The jets circled a six mile perimeter, using radar and camera visuals, but there was nothing.

"You guys seeing anything back there?" Stoddard asked, referring to the video monitors on the ship.

"We got squat, save for millions of gallons of salt water," Karnes said.

"I think somebody hacked into the Coast Guard's communications, sir," Stoddard said, "'cause there sure isn't anything out here."

"We've got confirmed reports from North-Atlantic cruises. They were in communication with the vessel until the distress call and haven't heard a peep from the ship since."

"What was that?" Banks said, eyeing the small LCD screen in the cockpit.

"What?" Stoddard asked. "You see Godzilla's head poking out of the water?"

"No, looked like a giant purple-colored whale breached the surface for a second."

"Ha. Ha." Karnes said. "If there's nothing there, get your asses back to the ship. We can't be wasting valuable fuel, and we have a schedule to keep. We'll let the Coast Guard handle it from here."

"Wait a sec, sir," the communications officer said. "I think that's debris in the water."

Karnes leaned closer to one of the monitors as the video was backed up a few frames, then set to play on slow. The image was also zoomed in on. "Shit. That is debris, and are those . . ."

Silence.

"What is it, sir?" Stoddard asked, hearing concern in the man's voice.

"We've got a visual on debris and body parts."

Silence filled the air for a few seconds, then, "Looks like we have a situation here. Possible terrorist threat." Karnes had the communications officer radio the nearest fleet and the Coast Guard, and report their findings.

"Stoddard and Banks, get your asses back here on the double."

"Holy shit, did you see that?" Banks yelled.

"Oh, my Lord," Stoddard said.

The creature rose from the water, arms and tentacles outstretched. Its roar was heard over the jets' engines. The fighters circled back around to get a better look at it.

"Sir, are you getting this?" Banks asked.

"What in the holy hell is that?" Lieutenant Commander Karnes asked.

"What do we do?" Stoddard said.

The lieutenant got the captain on the radio, the man in his cabin. "Sir, we need you up on the bridge, now. We've got a . . . situation."

Only glimpses of the creature were sent back to the ship until the pilots targeted the cameras at the creature, allowing the cameras on both aircraft to keep visuals on the thing regardless if the plane was facing it or not.

The creature turned this way and that, following them with its stare.

"I think we should kill it before it does something," Banks said.

"Hell yeah," Stoddard said. "What are our orders, sir? I don't think this thing is friendly."

"Hold for the captain unless you are engaged."

The creature groped at one of the planes as it flew near, but the Hornet was too fast and just out of its reach.

"That was close," Stoddard said, able to keep an eye on Banks' jet.

The creature roared again, seeming angry, and when the jets flew by the thing again, a tentacle shot forward and clipped the Sidewinder missile on Banks' left wing. The weapon came free and was in the monster's grip.

Alarms went off in Banks' cockpit. "Holy shit, I think it just hit me."

"It did," Stoddard said.

"But we aren't close enough," Banks said.

"It's got long-ass tentacles. Damn thing just shot from its body like Spiderman's web shooter," Stoddard said.

"Get back. Disengage the target, but hold the area," Karnes said.

The missile finally exploded as the creature hung onto it. It cried out for a second, the sound seeming more like surprise than hurt. The winged critters that scurried around the large beast shrieked as they took flight and headed for Banks' aircraft when he came back around at the monster.

"Watch out," Stoddard yelled, seeing the swarm of winged serpents shoot toward Banks. But it was too late. The small creatures were fast and on target, like guided organic missiles.

Banks shrieked. "What the hell? I can't see." He hit the afterburner and took off, but the creatures were latched onto his plane. "Can't shake them."

Stoddard wanted to help his friend, but there was nothing he could do.

***

The winged creatures sank their claws into Bank's jet, piercing the metal. A few couldn't hang on due to the overwhelming speed, but most did. Their sucker mouths latched onto the cockpit's glass shield as well as the plane's wings. Banks looked up and saw an orange-colored secretion coming from the serpents' mouths. The glass was sizzling and dissolving, the serpents' saliva like acid. As the cockpit was breached, it filled with the scent of ammonia and some other chemical smell he couldn't identify. Seconds after the wind poured in, so did the serpents. They were on him, covering him like wet blankets. He yanked one free from his head and pulled away part of his scalp with it. The serpent was as thick and as heavy as a rolled up Oriental carpet. It simply latched onto his shoulder, making his arm useless.

***

"They're inside the . . . cockpit. All over me," Banks screamed. "Hurts bad. Some kind of acid eating through everything."

"Eject, Banks. Eject," Stoddard yelled.

The next thing he saw was Banks sailing skyward, a dark, plum-colored mass surrounding him in cocoon-like fashion. There were still serpents attached to the fighter plane as it crashed into the ocean. Banks' parachute opened and he descended slowly until the strings snapped.

"Kill . . . me . . ." Banks muttered as he plummeted toward the water.

The behemoth lurched toward him. A tentacle shot forth and snatched Banks from the air. The winged serpents took flight and returned to the behemoth, where they settled back along its flesh, as if home again.

Banks made no sounds as he was brought to the starfish-shaped orifice and devoured, the visual like a crumb going into a giant's mouth.

"Oh, my God," the communications officer said over the comms.

Captain Lankford had come onto the bridge during the spectacle, having been updated about the situation by Lieutenant Commander Karnes.

"Blow that thing to hell," Lankford ordered. "Launch everything you have at it." He then gave the order for the ship to ready battle stations, and to get more planes in the air.

Stoddard was scared. Swallowing was nearly impossible. He needed a drink. His best friend, a man he considered like a brother, had just been killed. They lived next door to each other. Their wives were best friends. This whole ally-touring thing was supposed to be safe, the last mission before they retired and lived the good life down in the Florida Keys under the sun while they sold Margaritas to out-of-towners.

As shocked and afraid as he was, he had a job to do and a person to avenge. The creature was huge. He wasn't sure if the weapons he had were enough to kill it, but maybe a direct shot to the head would bring it down, or at least weaken it. Hell, maybe it was weaker than it appeared, like a jellyfish—fierce in appearance, but physically not much.

He flew back around and came at the creature head on. It turned and faced him, its mass of tentacles wriggling about like the snakes that made up Medusa's hair. The starfish thing on its chest pulsed, then opened and closed like an oddly shaped mouth. *No, not like a mouth, it is a mouth. It's where Banks had gone.*

He targeted the monster's head, and then launched a few missiles. The explosive-carrying projectiles flew away as he fired his machine guns, sending 20mm bullets at the thing. Tentacles shot forward and struck the missiles the way a frog snatches flies from the air. They exploded upon impact and didn't come near the creature. The bullets appeared to do nothing, the monster showing no sign that it was under duress.

More tentacles came from the creature's sides and torso, heading straight for him. He banked a sharp right and hit the afterburner, not wanting to get tangled up. When he was clear of the monster's reach, he circled back, targeted the beast and fired more missiles.

The tentacles intercepted all four.

"Are you seeing this, Captain?" Stoddard asked.

"Affirmative. Keep it in your sights, but do not engage. We're sending additional aircraft your way. We'll get this thing."

Stoddard flew in a circular pattern around the creature, slowly leading it toward the soon-to-be approaching flight of fighter jets. His pulse was still racing and he couldn't stop thinking about Banks. The man was dead, killed by some gargantuan creature; an alien for all he knew. He wondered where it had come from, but realized none of that mattered now. Let the scientists study its corpse when it was dead. As far as Banks went, he could mourn his friend when the time was right. He needed to keep his head in the game, stay alert, for the monster was obviously dangerous and had an assortment of attacks.

It moved fast through the water and Stoddard had to keep flying farther and farther away. He wasn't about to take a chance and let it get too close.

"We've got you and the creature on radar," the ship reported. "Hang in there. Help should be there momentarily."

He thought about his wife and kids, and how he needed to get back to them, but he also had a job to do and humanity to keep safe. He couldn't imagine the devastation the creature would cause if it ever reached land. Thousands, maybe even millions, would die. He couldn't allow that to happen.

Finally, two squadrons arrived on the scene, twelve planes in total. Flight Commander Lieutenant Jeffries was in charge of both groups. Stoddard felt the hairs on his arms and neck stand tall at seeing the backup arrive and knowing how much firepower was available. The creature wouldn't stand a chance. As huge as it was, it was still flesh.

Stoddard circled around and fell in line with the formation.

Gasps, curses and prayers sounded over the comm units as the creature came into view.

"Gentlemen," Jeffries said, "it's big and ugly and who the hell knows what else, but we've got enough firepower to level a few cities and then some. We're going to make this quick so we can all get back to our families. Focus on the job. You've all been trained by the best. Think about it later."

"Damn," Jimenez said, "that's one ugly son of a bitch."

"Some kind of demon from hell, I think," Danvers said, and Stoddard could picture the man crossing himself.

"Whatever it is, it's going down," Stoddard said. "For Banks."

"For Banks," was echoed over the comms.

"This thing's nasty," Stoddard warned. "Has a lot of tricks. Don't get too close. It's got an army of tentacles and winged serpents, and it's fast for its size."

"We're not here to hug the thing, folks," Jimenez said. "Blow it to hell and thank you for coming to the show."

The now single squadron fanned out into attack formation as it came into targeting range. The plan was simple: everyone fire at the same time so the creature couldn't intercept all the missiles. Then, the creature did something they hadn't counted on—it dove underwater and disappeared.

"Shit," someone said.

"The target has submerged," Jeffries said. "No visual."

"We've got it on radar," the communications officer back on the ship said. "It's damn huge."

As the squad continued onward, it flew straight over the area where the creature had been.

"Must've frightened it off," Jimenez said.

Stoddard didn't think so. More likely, it had a higher form of intelligence—ape or dolphin level—and was smarter than they all knew. Somehow, it had sensed the danger.

"Thing's a pus—" Jimenez started.

Hundreds of gallons of salt water shot upward as the monster burst from the depths. Tentacles shot at the squad and struck six of the twelve jets. Three of the aircraft exploded on impact, while damaged others spiraled out of control. Trails of black smoke streamed behind. Screams erupted over the comm units as pieces of steel, tail wings and rockets decorated the air. The men ejected almost in unison. As their planes splashed into the ocean, they were snatched out of the air by the creature's long-reaching tentacles, their parachutes not even getting a chance to open.

"Climb, climb, climb," ordered Jeffries.

"Holy shit," Jimenez said. "That thing just wiped out half of us."

Each plane had been fitted with a camera, allowing the men on the carrier's bridge to see what was going on.

The remaining squadron flew high and away before it turned around and came at the creature. The monster was focused on them and roared as it threw its arms out wide. Its eel-tongue lashed and swayed, like a cobra caught in a snake charmer's musical rhythm.

Stoddard swallowed hard, the lump in his throat feeling like a rock that wouldn't go down. The creature was like something from a child's nightmare, brought into the world of men by sheer will.

"Lock-on, gentlemen, and fire at will," Jeffries said.

Missiles took flight, each one targeted on various parts of the creature. As expected, tentacles shot out and intercepted the attack. The precision was incredible and awe-inspiring. The monster's long tail whipped out of the water, creating a tidal wave of oceanic-wrath, and swatted at a group of missiles heading towards its head and chest with the giant-sized lobster claw attached at the end. The armed projectiles exploded on impact. When the smoke cleared, no visible damage to the behemoth could be seen.

Silence filled the comms, and Stoddard knew everyone was in shock. As the squadron pulled up and away, making sure to stay out of the creature's range, Jimenez spoke.

"That ain't right. That just ain't right."

"What are we going to do?" Danvers asked.

"Not one damn missile got through," Stoddard said, stating the obvious.

"Okay," Jeffries said, and Stoddard could hear the strain in the man's voice. "New plan of attack. Jimenez, Stoddard and I will come at the thing from the north side. Jackson, Danvers and Burns from the south. When we're all locked on, we light that thing up."

"Sounds like a plan," Stoddard said, anxious to know if the creature could, in fact, be harmed.

The squadron split into two groups, three planes in each, and flew in opposite directions away from the beast. About a mile out, they turned around and headed straight at the creature.

Stoddard's stomach was doing summersaults and his skin was lined with sweat. Clammy hands filled his gloves and his brow was soaked.

The planes were like flies to the behemoth, their weapons mere annoyances that couldn't even make contact with its body. Stoddard didn't think their weapons would be enough to stop it, but they had orders to follow, and they had to try something. If they could wound it, make it bleed, then he and the others would feel a hell of a lot better. They could then call in bigger guns and take it out before . . .

He hadn't thought much more than beyond the *now*. He suddenly wondered where the creature had come from and if there were more. The ocean was vast and deep. Most of it still remained unexplored and was unreachable. Maybe the thing had come from outer space and was part of some invading alien race. A first wave of the invading force sent to test and take out human defenses. The truth was that he had no idea what the creature was or where it came from, and he couldn't afford to spend the mental power thinking about such things now. Stoddard shook the thoughts from his mind. He was being ridiculous, but then again, he realized he wasn't. This thing wasn't supposed to be possible, but here it was in the flesh.

"Target locked," Jeffries said.

Stoddard and the other men echoed the statement. They needed to make sure everyone fired at the same time.

"Let's send this thing to the bottom of the ocean," Jeffries said. "Fire."

Missiles sailed away from both groups of fighter planes and left white smoky trails behind. The squads then banked left and sped away, letting the weapons do their thing.

Tentacles lashed out, intercepting missiles. Explosions crackled the air like dull-looking fireworks. Pieces of tentacle blew apart, the more powerful missiles causing more damage. The creature's blood, a bright glowing purple goo, seeped from the wounds like molasses. The injured tentacles receded into the creature from where they came and new sucker-lined appendages shot out and took their place.

The creature used its clawed tail as a shield and blocked a barrage of missiles that came at it from behind, then it whipped it around and batted away a second attack. Winged serpents also joined in, acting as living shields. The things swarmed the airspace around the behemoth, like gnats on a hot summer night. Legs, heads and wings were blown apart, but there were so many that it didn't seem to matter.

Eventually, by the fourth go round, a few missiles got through. One hit the monster just below the right eye. Another detonated against its outer thigh, and a third exploded across a part of its lower back. Its head had jerked slightly when the missile hit it in its face, revealing that it at least was surprised, but Stoddard figured it was more likely that it had felt some sort of pain. The creature roared and thrashed about, almost tantrum-like, as if it were truly pissed off.

The squad continued to circle the beast from afar. The cameras were getting great footage of the monster. The men back on the ship had hoped to get an idea of the creature's weak spots or any damage, but so far, it didn't look like it had taken much. The behemoth's face, where it had taken the direct hit, looked slightly discolored, as if it had been slapped and not bombarded. Its thigh too was a darker shade of purple. Its hide was proving tough, and it was going to take more firepower to really hurt it.

"I think we're going to need bigger guns," Jimenez said.

"No shit," Danvers said. "Call in a few nukes."

"Hey, it looks like we irritated it, even hurt it a little," Jeffries said.

"You know the line," Jimenez said. "If it bleeds, we can kill it."

"This ain't no movie," Stoddard said. "But I hear you, Jimenez."

"It does look like we can harm it," Jeffries said. "Anything we can do now will help with how to properly take it down. It's got to have weak spots and I'm guessing those are where its armor comes together, as well as the softer-looking skin. Now, re-form into your groups and attack with whatever you have left."

The squad broke off into two groups again. The creature followed Jeffries' group for a few moments and then it stopped and held its arms out like a fighter's, as if readying to face off with them. It knew they were going to come back at it.

Stoddard didn't like it. The monster was clearly showing intelligence. It might be more prepared this time, had figured out its enemy a little better. Studied its prey. The situation was bad enough, but if the behemoth could think and plan, then they were all in more trouble than they imagined.

Most of the winged serpents that had taken flight had returned to the creature and were slithering across its body like maggots on a corpse. Then, like a flock of birds, they took flight again, but instead of hovering around the beast or coming at the attacking squadron, they dove into the ocean. The creature's fluorescent purple flesh shined brighter as it was no longer obstructed by wriggling snakes. Its form was more revealed now, allowing its carapace segmented body to be more clearly seen. The shell armor covered its chest and torso, shoulders, back, arms and legs, with spaces between sections of the armor, similar to a football player's protective gear.

"The thing's a giant purple lobster," Jimenez said.

"No wonder we hardly wounded it," Danvers said.

"Anyone else concerned that those flying snakes left its body?" Stoddard asked.

"Maybe we scared them off," Danvers said.

"Who knows, but they're gone," Jeffries said. "We stay the course. The creature's soft spots are clearer now, including that starfish opening. We target those areas."

The behemoth charged forward with incredible speed. Targeting sensors went off for the northbound group, but the south was out of range now.

"Shit," Jeffries said. "Fire."

"We aren't in range yet, sir," someone from the southbound group said.

"Shit, shit, shit," Stoddard said. "It's smart. It knows. Somehow it knows."

The creature lashed out with its massive clawed tail and swatted away the missiles like a hand to mosquitoes. Tentacles attacked, too. Nothing got through. The northbound squad pulled up and away as the creature neared. It leapt from the water, tentacles reaching and managed to latch onto Danvers' plane. He screamed in obvious fright, then ejected from the plane as it was deposited in the creature's hands. The monster made quick work of the 37,000 pound aircraft, crushing it in seconds and turning it to rubble.

As the southbound squad came into firing range, the water below them burst like an erupting volcano. The winged serpents flew up and into the three planes, blanketing them in a sheet of darkness. The fighter jets were battered and they quickly broke apart. The men didn't even have time to eject before their crafts burst into flames and scattered into the sea.

"No," Jimenez yelled.

"They ambushed us," Stoddard mumbled, hardly believing his words. "Fucking ambushed us."

Danvers was speaking into his headset, begging for someone to help him as he floated gently downward. There was nothing anyone could do for him. Stoddard could only hope the man would survive in the waters until help arrived. Then, a soul-shaking wail pierced the airwaves.

Danvers screamed as a tentacle wrapped around his body, seat and all. The tiny suckers latched onto him. The teeth made quick work of his flight suit and flesh, eating him down to muscle, then bone in moments, silencing his awful screams. The tentacles tossed what little remains were left into the starfish-shaped orifice on its chest.

Stoddard caught the end result on his small LCD screen and wondered, of all things, why the creature bothered with such a small meal.

"This is so—" Jimenez began.

"Keep your head on straight, pilot," Jeffries said. "We have a job to complete."

"Complete?" Jimenez asked, sounding bewildered. "There's nothing left to do but die, sir."

Stoddard agreed. They needed to get the hell out of there and regroup back at the ship. Figure something out. Wait for the cavalry.

The massive cloud of winged serpents flew back to their host and settled down, the creature's glowing skin darkening again.

The three remaining fighters gave the beast a wide berth as they circled around it. Anger coursed through Stoddard's veins. As frightened as he'd been, he was pissed now. He wanted more than anything else to kill this thing, launch a nuke at it if he had to. Zooming in on his cockpit's camera, he studied the creature, specifically where it had been hit. If he didn't know any better, he'd swear the discolored skin on the behemoth's face looked normal again.

The creature roared, as it swiveled in place, following the planes with its eyes. Stoddard wondered why it wasn't charging at them, trying to attack them, but was glad it wasn't. They were low on ammo, save for the 20mm bullets, but if missiles barely left a mark, then bullets were a waste of time. And no one was getting close enough to try.

"Captain," Jeffries said. "Please advise."

"Get back here on the double. I'm on the horn with the president. Help is on the way."

Stoddard was glad to hear it. They were heading back to safety. He wasn't prepared to give up, not in the least. He wanted to reload, take a breather, and then get another shot at that thing.

As they flew away, the creature roared and thrashed wildly, creating a hurricane-like storm around it. It was pissed, Stoddard thought. Actually angry.

A moment later, it dove into the ocean and was gone.

# CHAPTER 11

Stoddard and the others flew back to the carrier. The ship was buzzing with activity. Pilots were at the ready, anxious, intrigued, gung ho and nervous as talk and rumor about the sea creature spread. A few planes were in the air, circling the ship's perimeter while they waited on the arrival of the USS Freedom, a naval warship that had been off the coast of Virginia. Normally, during times of war, carriers were guarded by a fleet of warships, but the USS Gauntlet's mission—though armed—had been one of peace and for show, so to speak.

Stoddard, Jeffries and Jimenez were debriefed soon after landing. The creature was no longer on radar, and the prevailing thought among the brain trust was that it had gone deep.

Stoddard and Jimenez went to their bunks, where they showered and were supposed to decompress, but to stay ready. No one knew if or when the creature was going to rear its ugly head again.

Though the bunkroom where Stoddard and Jimenez spent their nights was supposed to be empty—for them to have some time to themselves—a large group of Navy personnel had made their way in and bombarded both men with questions. No one wanted to believe it was true, that a giant monster was not only real, but had practically wiped out two squadrons.

After both men told their tales, the room broke into complete silence for a few moments. The crowd then made small talk as they nodded and stared at their shoes, eyes full of sadness and disbelief. Then, something seemed to affect the room. The men's expressions turned angry, scowls decorating their faces. Narrowed eyes and pursed lips. Everyone wanted to get up in the air and have a go at the beast.

They of course didn't understand what they were going to be up against. The creature wasn't just enormous—as tall as a the Empire State Building and as thick as three of them put together—but it was rippled with muscles, intelligent and possessed an assortment of attacks equivalent to something from a science fiction movie.

Nevertheless, the loss of life was something that made members of the armed forces come together in a way like no other. They were a family, a brother/sisterhood.

When it came down to it, Stoddard was scared, but he wouldn't think for another second about going back up. If the beast came back, he'd want another shot at it.

After having been in their bunkroom for fifteen minutes, the Captain entered the room and cleared it out, ordering everyone to the hanger deck, allowing Stoddard and Jimenez to have some down time.

"At ease, men," Captain Saunders said, and both men relaxed their posture. "They're just curious. But they need to leave you two alone for the next twenty."

"It's all right, sir," Jimenez said. "Feels good to be able to talk about it. Warn the guys. Be the teacher for a change. They have no idea what they're getting into . . . if that thing comes back."

"I know it's been a hell of a day," Saunders said. "You two have seen some ungodly sights, from what I hear . . . But take this time for yourselves. Use it. Get that shit that's pent up inside out. Scream, hit, smash something. Let the sadness come, but make it brief. We have no idea where that thing is. We need men like you, especially you two, back in the air if it does show itself again. In the meantime, I'll keep the men out of here. You've got twenty to do whatever it is you need to do. Then I want you suited up and at the ready."

"Yes, sir," both men said in unison.

After Captain Saunders left, both men sat on their bunks. Stoddard laid back and tried to relax, but he wasn't able to and wound up sitting back up. His body felt like it was riddled with ants.

With the room cleared out and Jimenez quiet, Stoddard's mind was working overtime. Emotions, both highs and lows, were stabbing him. He thought about Banks and the other pilots who had died. He thought about his family and his own mortality and how close he'd come to dying. He felt like his mind was being ripped apart and his head was going to explode. His stomach flooded with an overabundance of acid. An unseen force was pushing against the back of his eyes from within.

"You okay?" Jimenez asked.

Stoddard couldn't talk and simply shook his head. If he opened his mouth, he was going to puke. The room was spinning, his mind unable to concentrate on anything. He was having a delayed reaction to what he'd gone through. Post traumatic stress. A massive anxiety attack. He looked around the room and focused on the other bunks. His eyes fell to the beds of the dead pilots. Those beds would remain unoccupied until the ship returned home and new personnel were assigned to them. He wondered how many people had slept in them over the years. How many had never returned home alive?

His stomach dropped, as if he'd been on a roller coaster. He shot to his feet, his face white as chalk.

"Dude, you look—" Jimenez began.

Stoddard took off running to the head, where he hurled the contents of his stomach into the toilet.

"That a boy," Jimenez said. "Get it all out now."

Stoddard gulped in air as he leaned over the bowl. The pressure in his head had lessened, as if whatever was inside had exited along with his vomit.

He reached up and flushed, then he stood and wiped his lips. He washed himself up in the sink before returning to his bunk, tired.

"Feeling better?" Jimenez asked.

Stoddard nodded.

"After seeing some serious shit, puking helps. It's like a temporary way for our bodies to get us feeling good quickly so we can function at our best. You know?"

Stoddard agreed.

"My body reacts faster, however. Don't tell anyone this, but I puked in the cockpit."

Stoddard laughed.

"I just feel bad for the cleanup guys."

Stoddard had barely enough strength to lie down without collapsing. He closed his eyes, hoping to catch a few minutes of sleep, but it didn't come. Images of the monster and his fellow wingmen dying kept flashing across his mind.

"I can't believe what happened today," he said, needing to talk.

"I know. It's unreal. I mean, what the hell was that thing?"

"You've got me . . . Some kind of alien or something. Who knows."

Jimenez exhaled audibly. "We might never find out, just like we never know why one person dies instead of another, except that it's all about being at the wrong place at the wrong time. Chance. That shit's enough to think about. Now I have to wonder about a giant monster? If there are more of them out there besides the one we fought? I mean, when word gets out to civilians, how are they going to sleep at night? How are they going to go about their normal routines knowing there's a monster out there waiting to smash them like ants?"

"Damn, Jimenez, you aren't helping me relax."

"Sorry," he said. "You know my trick to dealing with shit like this?"

"Puking?"

Jimenez laughed. "Well, besides that. I let a little in at a time. Think over stuff, but don't get too emotionally involved. It's like glancing at a picture, but only briefly. Then I shove it away. Put it in a box for later. We're supposed to be machines. Have to follow orders and keep each other safe. Watch each other's backs. Can't do that if my mind is elsewhere. Once we get home, when I retire, then I'll see a doc about all the shit I've been through. Work it all out so my family doesn't have to take the brunt, you know what I mean?"

"Yeah, I hear you." Stoddard was all in for that. He'd seen a shrink once. The woman had helped him deal with losing a friend who'd been killed in Iraq. He'd fought with himself for a while on whether to talk to someone or not. His father had always told him that a man dealt with problems on his own or with family. No one paid a "professional" to help them. Shrinks were all bullshit. Same as psychics and all those other nature-loving freaks. Nothing but snake oil salesmen. But Stoddard had been hurting so badly and was willing to try anything, so he opened himself up to the idea of a therapist. And thank goodness he did, because it helped. He was able to deal and move on. Jimenez was right. When they got back to shore, he was seeing the doc. Being part of a mission where almost all their fellow pilots had been killed, wasn't something a puking session was going to fix.

He couldn't imagine how his family would be if he died. How they'd survive. Move on. There would be so much pain for all. He'd bring a world of heartache to his wife and kids. His parents too, but they were former military, and as hard as it would be for them to lose a son, they'd understand. His father would say his death had been righteous because he had been serving his country. There was no prouder thing a man could do.

Thinking about his family made his stomach queasy. He needed to think of something else.

"I don't know how you block shit out," he said.

"It takes some practice. But our training . . . Being in the middle of the shit . . . It all helps. I tell myself that I can't do two things at once. I remember that I have a job to do, and if I don't do it, people will die. Stoddard wondered how he would feel if he didn't have a wife and kids. Would he think differently? Care less? Be more reckless when he flew? Have a different set of priorities?

He'd be the same person he was, he imagined. It was just seeing that creature wipe them all out . . . It was terrifying. He might not make it home if it came back.

Damn, his mind was reeling again. He needed to calm down and focus.

He sat up, ground his teeth, made a fist with his right hand and smacked it into his left.

"What gives?"

"We need to kill that thing. Sitting around here isn't doing anyone any good, least of all, me."

"Hell, yeah. I want to get up in the air and nuke that sucker."

Though he still felt uneasy, maybe even able to puke again, he kept himself in check. He swallowed, and mentally shoved his trepidation and doubt down into his gut. A rock felt like it was sitting at the bottom of his stomach, but so be it. He focused on himself and on his men. Nothing else mattered, except the present. Screw the creature and where it had come from. The only thing that counted now was finding and killing it.

# CHAPTER 12

The behemoth dove deep, to depths that would crush a human in seconds. It snatched up various forms of sea life, from sharks, to squid and octopus, to whales, lobsters and crabs, adding them all to its mass. It consumed everything it came across, breaking the prey down and absorbing the parts, as it had the humans, using their brains and their knowledge to help it learn about them.

As it ate, it healed what insignificant damage it had sustained. Its tentacles mended. Its flesh and armor were renewed. It didn't fully understand why it had gone so deep, for the humans couldn't hurt it in the water, but somehow it knew it needed to go that far down. It knew the humans could not travel to such depths. It was safe down there, where sunlight could not go and things dwelled in the darkness.

The humans would come after it. They would hunt it until they killed it, never giving up. The behemoth could not allow that to happen, not before it had its vengeance.

Images of Vinnie flashed across its mind, like a bolt of lightning brightening the night sky. With the sight came immense pain. The loss the creature felt was overwhelming, the sadness devastating. It cried out, thrashed and kicked, and broke off a rather large piece of ocean rock that had formed a cliff over a ravine. The plateau-like chunk fell and shattered, sending smaller pieces into the cavernous crack where they disappeared like childhood memories.

Mankind was evil, the creature thought. A disease to the planet. They were unnatural—like itself. It knew it existed because of mankind, and now its creator—however unintentional—was going to try to kill it, as they had so many other wonderful things in the world.

But it had a focused purpose, a goal to accomplish before it took on the world. Vinnie needed to be put down, along with his goons, Johnny and Scottie. The behemoth would make sure they all suffered, but none more than Vinnie, the man in charge.

The creature fought its emotions, wanting all of mankind to suffer for the atrocities that they caused the world, but at the same time, it knew they weren't all bad. In fact, most were good. It remembered being human, that part of it still very much alive. But at the same time, it was no longer only human. It was a hybrid, a mixed breed of creature that no other creatures would accept. It would always be alone.

The creature thrashed its tail and shattered an outcropping of coral reef, sending hundreds of small critters racing about, scurrying for new homes and for safety. It reached out with its tentacles and snatched up as many as it could.

The creature needed to get revenge for its former family, the ones it had once loved. It would kill all that tried to stop it from getting its revenge, from killing Vinnie.

But then what? What would it do and where would it go when Vinnie was dead? Would it really attempt to wipe mankind from the planet? It didn't know. It would worry about such things later. For now, it needed to figure out how to find Vinnie.

The location appeared in its mind: NYC. The human part of it had lived there. New York City was a place with tall buildings and millions of humans. The creature saw the world in its mind and knew where it had to go. The military humans would try to stop it, but they were no match for it. It would wipe them all out, and then proceed to New York City.

The humans above were on a ship. A dangerous ship, not like the one it had destroyed. This one had weapons, but no flying craft. Regardless, the human vessel would be no match for the creature.

It roared angrily. It was done hiding. They couldn't hurt it, not really.

With a thrust of its legs, it shot upward at incredible speed, pumping its arms and legs, muscles bulging. A few moments later, it breached the surface. The humans were gone. It sniffed the air, saw the smoky jet trails, and knew which way to go.

# CHAPTER 13

Stoddard was back in his flight suit and heading for the flight deck when the *all hands on deck* alarm sounded. He knew it could only mean that the creature was on its way toward the ship, or at least that it was close by.

Fighter planes were being launched, the flight deck a symphony of jet engines. He knew his bird wasn't going to be ready, but he'd be damned if he was going to wait around. He had to be in the sky, the captain had said so. He found the flight officer who was in charge, and the man immediately had him in a fighter jet right behind Jimenez and Jeffries.

The fly buddies were in the air minutes later. Stoddard had received word that the creature was indeed heading straight for the carrier. The ship didn't have much in the way of weapons to defend itself with—no missiles or heavy machine guns—save the aircraft on board. The fighter planes were going to be the only thing standing between the ship and the monster, and they would have to do so until either, they killed it or help arrived. A warship was en route and only minutes away. Another carrier was twenty miles out and had two more warships with it.

Stoddard had never seen so many planes in the air, especially during a combat mission. There were four squads, making up a flight of twenty-four planes, for the first wave of attack. With this much firepower, Stoddard thought, they should be able to kill the monstrosity.

They flew side by side in two lines of twelve, one group above the other—an uncommon formation to go along with the uncommon enemy.

As the creature came into view, it saw the planes and stopped. It came to an upright position. Its size seemed even larger. Murmurs sounded over the comms. People breathed heavy, swore or prayed. They'd all heard about it, but seeing it was something else—brought the thing to life.

Jeffries was the squadron commander of all twenty-four aircraft. More planes were launching from the ship and forming into yet another squad that would act as an immediate second wave of attack, a blitzkrieg. The idea was to not allow the creature time to recover. They were going to overwhelm the hell out of it.

Targets were locked, and the creature roared in unison, as if accepting the gauntlet and ready to do battle.

Missiles flew, streams of white smoke filling the sky. The planes banked left and right, going around the creature and making sure to keep out of its reach.

The behemoth lashed out with its tentacles, and there were new-looking ones this time. They looked like a squid's—long, thin stalks that led to wider, suction cup ends. Both kinds of appendages worked together, and it seemed like the thing had twice as many.

Some of the missiles simply broke apart and crashed into the sea, while others detonated upon impact with the creature's tentacles. Explosions riddled the air. The giant lobster clawed tail came into play and whipped about, blocking a group of missiles. Winged serpents took flight, kamikazing themselves into missiles. All in all, it didn't look like much got through, if anything, and a radio report from the ship confirmed it.

"Shit," Jeffries said. "Re-form. This time, we approach from behind it while the second wave comes from the other side. We'll get this thing sooner or later."

"Roger that," said the second squad's leader.

As both teams of aircraft came in, targets were locked and missiles were fired. Winged serpents were already out front, taking out half the attack, their sleek black bodies turned into flaming barbeque. Tentacles went to work and burst apart as detonation occurred. There was no way to tell how many tentacles the thing had, but eventually, they'd burn through them all and leave the monster much more defenseless. A few missiles got through, exploding on the creature's arms and back, but it didn't seem to bother the thing.

"Fly out and re-form," Jeffries said. "We keep hitting it until its dead or we're out of ammo."

The groups came in again, firing a multitude of missiles. A cacophony of explosions occurred in front of and behind the creature. Most of the attack had been thwarted, but a small number of missiles hit their intended targets. The behemoth's shell-like armor seemed to take no damage, the stuff unchanged in its appearance. But the missiles that hit the softer-looking areas—the gaps of flesh between its bicep and shoulder and upper and lower back just above the tail—appeared to do harm. The flesh was split in a few places. Small gashes were leaking a purple substance, which had to be the creature's blood.

The planes re-formed into their respective groups and came back again, launching a barrage of missiles. All craft targeted the fleshy spots, as well as the head. The creature blocked most of the attacks, the tentacles and serpents seemingly in endless supply, but Stoddard, along with everyone else's spirits, soared at seeing the monster take damage—and not a single human casualty had occurred. It was early in the fight, he knew, but it was a good sign.

The air attack kept on. For every twelve missiles fired, maybe two got through the tentacle/winged-serpent/lobster claw-tail defense, and most of the time, only the armored areas were hit. The beast was moving around more, lunging at the squads as they came at the thing, trying to snatch the jet fighter planes out of the sky. After a few go rounds, Stoddard noticed how the hard, shiny armor began to change color after a weapon detonated against it. The purple shell darkened to an almost onyx color and rippled outward from the point of impact, like the wave effect from a stone dropping into a calm body of water. He wondered if it meant that the creature's armor was breaking down, and if the beast itself was feeling the pain, weakening. Eventually, maybe the armor would crack and leave the behemoth much more exposed. But there was no way to know what was happening to the armor, so in the meantime, the soft spots were still the main targets.

More and more planes came from the ship and joined in on the attack. With coordination from the ship, mid-air collisions were avoided, though it was getting a little crowded in the skies.

During his last fly by, Stoddard noticed that some of the wounds had stopped bleeding and a scab of some kind had formed. The damn thing was restoring itself. "We have to keep aiming for the wounds," he said. "We need to keep it from healing."

With more planes in the air, Jeffries decided that a new attack pattern was needed in hopes of further overwhelming the creature.

Instead of the fighter planes attacking in smaller groups, one group attacking right after the other, the aircraft formed into two large groups and attacked at one time from two sides. Planes targeted high and low in hopes of overwhelming the monster. The creature took more hits and appeared frustrated as well as confused. It thrashed around, then wildly lunged at the planes and swung its tail in great, swooping arcs, but never came close enough to take any out. Even with the blitzkrieg assault, the creature hardly looked ready to die even though it was clearly taking more damage. Its ability to heal so quickly was of great concern, but this new plan of attack would hopefully be a solution to that problem.

Stoddard saw that they were finally turning the tide, winning, and as long as the behemoth didn't run, they might have a chance to bring it down with a lucky shot to the head or some other vital organ. They just needed to keep up the assault and hope the creature was too stupid and angered to flee.

# CHAPTER 14

The behemoth growled as it swiped at the air with its long arms, its ten-foot long claws, unable to reach any of the aircraft. Its tentacles were busy defending itself, not that they would've been able to grab any of the humans anyway. The tiny attackers were proving formidable, even dangerous in larger numbers. The source was up ahead. The planes were coming from the ship, like bees from a nest. Like its own parts, the humans seemed to be infinite in number. More and more were joining the assault and attacking it, hurting it. Half of its tentacles were damaged, half of that number useless. It needed to do something, needed to stop the source of the attack.

The eel tongue shot out as a group of planes flew by. The large serpent didn't come close to the crafts, but it wasn't meant to. Instead, the tongue-serpent opened its mouth and spewed a stream of orange-colored acid, hitting four planes and dissolving them to a sludge that rained into the water below. A fifth plane lost a wing and spiraled away, leaving a black-smoky trail behind before it crashed into the water.

More missiles collided with the creature. New wounds formed and old ones reopened. Its ability to heal was significantly slowed. The eel tongue's acid would take time to regenerate, and using it against a relentless swarm was going to take to much time. The monster refused to run. It would defeat the enemy before returning to the depths to heal, and then it would head for one of the largest hubs of humanity and bring the city to its knees.

The behemoth needed to stop the source of the aircraft, and then it could begin to take them all out.

Snorting in disgust, for its fleeing would only be temporary, it went under and raced to depths where no human could travel and where their machines could not reach nor see it. They were so small, weak-fleshed and easily killed. But they were thinkers, creators, and at the top of the food chain. That was all going to change now that it existed.

The creature reached the ocean floor, gobbling up sea life as it went, feeding and replenishing itself. It then grabbed handfuls of rock and crushed it into hundreds of smaller stones as it swam back to the surface, its target in sight.

# CHAPTER 15

"Damn it," Jeffries said. "It went under." He ordered everyone to pull up. "Command, do you have eyes on the target?"

"We did for a few seconds, but it's gone. It went deep."

"Must've scared it off," someone said.

"That's right," someone else said. "Damn thing ain't so tough."

"No," Stoddard said harshly. "We barely hurt it. It was healing as we were fighting it. That thing was far from done. We've seen it do some tricky stuff. It dove on us before, only to come back and wipe most of us out. Don't relax and don't get sloppy. This thing is intelligent and a killer."

"He's right, men," Jeffries said. "It may be off radar, but that doesn't mean it's gone. We stay the course and wait."

The two super-sized squads—now composed of twenty-six planes each—circled the area in a four-mile perimeter. The carrier continued to search for the monster on radar. The airwaves were quiet for a while, the silence unnerving and unwelcomed. It was like the quiet before a devastating storm, the kind of tempest that flooded entire towns and brought down buildings, Stoddard thought. Despite his trepidation, he was pissed. The creature was healing now that it wasn't taking damage, and again, he knew as long as they were at sea, it wasn't going to go down, short of a sub hitting it with a nuke.

Part of him hoped it had run off, scared and hurt. This would give them time for more ships to arrive. More firepower meant more of a chance they could kill the thing. Even launch a nuke at it if they had to. He couldn't imagine what would happen if it reached land, a major city no less. They'd have a better chance of killing it there. It wouldn't be able to dive, but there would be far more casualties.

"It's back," came the communication officer's voice over the headsets.

"Location?" Jeffries asked.

"Shit, it's right below us."

Stoddard felt the hairs stand tall on his neck, as his flesh grew cold. It was going for the carrier.

"It's coming in fast," the man said, his voice panicked.

Stoddard couldn't believe it. If he hadn't been certain before, he was now—the thing was smart. Once it took out the ship, its enemy wouldn't be able to keep attacking it in numbers, especially once it started taking them out, like it had the four already.

As the aircraft raced back toward the ship, Stoddard, along with everyone else, knew they were going to have a fight on their hands. A close-up battle, with the ship and its crew as the hostages. They were going to have to hit the creature hard, attack it with as much force as ever while avoiding hitting the ship.

"Brace for impact," the communications officer shouted, and Stoddard knew there wasn't going to be a ship to protect.

The carrier shot out of the water as if a bomb had gone off below it. But instead of an explosion, it was the creature, the ship resting on its wide shoulder. The behemoth had smashed into it like a linebacker does a quarterback who's still holding onto the football. The hull snapped, pieces splintering away as if it was nothing more than a plastic toy. Planes that had been on deck twirled into the air like tops, and tiny stick figures waved their arms and legs as they sailed across the sky.

The creature continued upward, its hands balled into fists, tentacles whipping about like some crazy guitar player's hair.

"Fire," Jeffries yelled, and that seemed to break the shock and awe everyone, including Stoddard, had been caught in. Missiles fired, but unlike before, Stoddard felt no sense of power, as if the attacks were meaningless and a waste of time. But they had to do something. Jeffries was a good leader, acting the way a leader should despite whatever else was going on.

Men hollered, swore and screamed as the missiles flew.

The carrier was gone. Over four thousand men and women dead or would be, and the creature had done it all in seconds. The sea was its territory, a place it would have dominance. As far as Stoddard could see, they'd never be able to bring it down out here, short of a sub coming along with a few nukes.

The creature descended, splashing into the sea. The locked-on missiles followed, exploding harmlessly into the water.

Jeffries ordered the squad to climb; not wanting to take a chance the monster could attack them.

"What the hell do we do now?" someone asked.

"We stay the course," Jeffries said. "Do our job. Kill the damn thing."

"Are you nuts?" another person asked.

"Did you see what that thing did?" said another.

"We're safe in the air, men. I need you to hold it together for a bit longer. Until we take this thing out. Then you can go home and cry to your mommies. But until then, I'm ordering everyone here to stay the course and send that damn thing back to hell."

"But . . . we lost . . . the carrier," someone said, and Stoddard recognized the voice as officer Kelner's, the man a six-foot-eight muscled giant who was as tough as they come.

"Yeah, really," said Hanks, another pilot from Stoddard's bunk. "Where are we going to land when we run out of fuel?"

"There's another carrier sixty miles south of here," Jeffries said. "They were en route to us as soon as word got out about the monster. There's also a warship a couple miles out. We're not alone in this, men. Help is on the way. Stay together and focused until the mission is done."

The creature emerged from the water. The squads formed into tighter groups and circled the beast, staying out of its reach. Stoddard's nerves were fried, his mind running with thoughts and images of his dead shipmates and the future—if he'd have one. He knew the other men were thinking the same thing. It's what humans did in times of stress, but the key was to not do it for long.

He was caught in an emotional bundle of dynamite, ready to explode. The pressure behind his eyes was great, like a balloon was being inflated inside his head. But he kept himself in check and shoved those headache-inducing and stomach-churning feelings way down deep. When this was all over with, he was going to have one hell of a psych report.

He looked out his cockpit window and saw the plethora of fighter planes. Whether he believed it or not, he had to tell himself they had the firepower to bring the creature down, or at the very least, to let it definitely know they meant business. Maybe it would learn, like most animals, to stay away from humans.

He glanced toward the monster and watched it turn in accordance with the circling squad of aircraft. It was studying them, waiting to see what they were going to do. Maybe it was looking for weaknesses. He hoped that it seeing so many craft in the air, that it was plagued with indecision and fear. He wanted it to be afraid, but at the same time, he wanted it to be fearless so that it would stay and fight. Then they could kill it.

Stoddard didn't want to think it was intelligent, not like a human, but he feared it was. It had taken out the carrier, recognized the source of its attackers. It was a wise move.

Regardless, they were in the air and as long as they remained out of the thing's grasp, they'd be okay.

Half the planes flew out north, the other half to the south. The plan was the same: attack from two sides and overwhelm the hell out of the beast until more help arrived. They knew to keep an eye out for if and when the winged serpents dove into the water or took flight, and knew to watch out for the acid-spewing tongue. Unless it had more tricks up its sleeve, Stoddard thought the remaining squads should be all right.

Despite his reassurances to himself, Stoddard was numb. He'd succeeded at turning off his emotions, leaving him a hollow shell. He couldn't believe all that had happened today. All the death and destruction, and of course, that there was a skyscraper-sized monster about. It was impossible to wrap his mind around it all. Even to fathom such a beast was unreal. Truth be told, he didn't want to be able to comprehend it all. If he did, his mind might crack, and he couldn't afford to lose his marbles now. None of the men could. Together, they stood a chance of getting out of this situation alive.

"As soon as we're all locked on, we fire at will," Jeffries said, speaking to the entire company of aircraft and breaking Stoddard from his thoughts.

As they drew near the beast, targeting systems locking on, the monster cocked back its right arm, then threw it forward. Its clenched hand opened when its arm was fully extended and it released a bundle of debris that flew through the air like buckshot.

"Incoming!" Jeffries yelled.

Planes banked left and right, hoping to avoid the attack, but the debris was too plentiful and spread out. The rock tore into a number of the aircraft, shredding hulls, tearing off wings and smashing into cockpits. Pilots were obliterated, crushed like bugs on a windshield. A couple of planes exploded. Men's screams were quickly silenced. A couple of jets collided with each other during the confusion, as everyone tried to bank in different directions. The sky was total chaos. Thinking that down was the best place to go, Stoddard shoved the yoke forward. The Hornet dove. As the sea approached, he banked a hard left and hit the afterburner, fleeing the scene.

The squadron of aircraft coming in from behind the creature didn't know what to make of the attack on their brethren. Their course of action remained the same and missiles were launched. The creature spun in their direction, its other hand still balled into a fist, but only for a moment. It threw the debris it held in that hand at the incoming planes and their missiles. Explosions riddled the air as missiles were thwarted. The few that made it past the barrage of rock were met by tentacles.

Like its incoming northbound counterpart, the group of planes scattered, bumping into each other and getting torn apart by the projectile rock. Screams echoed over the comms. Men ejected, only to be met with death as rock and tentacle ripped them apart.

As the planes scattered about and headed away from the creature, Jeffries reminded the men to focus and stay on course. They quickly re-formed into their respective squads, finding that a third of their brothers were gone, and that the behemoth had gone under again.

A small number of parachutes were in the air, some with limp forms hanging from them. The living were calling out, begging for help. Some sounded like they were in immense pain, others just scared. As they hit the water, they were snatched under by the creature. The tentacles had been visible for only a moment when the octopus and squid arms wrapped themselves around the men. The silence left behind on the comms was haunting and louder than any explosion ever heard.

Jeffries informed the incoming warship about what had happened. Stoddard didn't think it was a good idea for any more watercraft to venture onto the scene. The creature was simply too powerful at sea. But he knew something had to be done. The men aboard the warship had no idea what they were getting themselves into. Stoddard could only hope the squadrons of aircraft would be able to bring the creature down before the warship arrived, and if that didn't happen, then he had to hope their combined efforts would kill the creature before it had a chance to attack the ship, like it had the carrier.

As the planes flew in their particular formations, the creature emerged. Its hands were balled into fists again. Someone alerted the aircraft to the fact, and everyone climbed higher, but not before the monster struck. It threw another shotgun-like rock attack at the south side squad and destroyed five more planes.

The rest of the company was away and safe. They then circled back around and headed straight for the creature. It remained where it was, waiting. No one wanted to engage it, not with it holding another handful of debris, but they couldn't take the chance it would depart if they didn't attack it. A small number of fighter planes flew at it and launched missiles, while the rest remained back. The creature held its fist closed and used its tentacles to take out the few missiles that targeted it, saving its handheld haul for when more planes attacked it.

Finally, the warship came into firing range of the beast. Radio contact was made and a coordinated attack plan was formed. The two squads came at the creature from opposite sides while the USS Ford launched its attack.

The creature hurled its remaining load at the southbound approaching squad. The planes flew high and away while the northbound squad attacked. The warship joined in, launching cruise missiles and torpedoes and firing rocket propelled warheads from its deck guns.

The creature spun on the approaching planes, tentacles lashing out, intercepting the attack. It didn't see the ship's attack and was hit in the back of the head, shoulders and arms. Then it stumbled and roared in what appeared to be pain as the sea around its torso exploded upwards—the torpedoes had struck. The water was a murky purple; the creature was bleeding.

"We have direct hits," came a voice from the ship.

The planes circled around and were coming back in for another attack.

Stoddard was able to see the back of the beast. The purple armor was speckled with dark spots. Ripples were breaking out from where it had been hit and it looked like small cracks had formed throughout the bombarded areas. The softer parts of its flesh were oozing small rivulets of purple blood. Stoddard felt his chest expand with pride. The creature was still a ways off from being defeated, but it was proving mortal and was in no way indestructible.

The planes locked on to targets and fired. The warship joined in the assault, the deck gun sounding like a crack of thunder and the cruise missiles being launched shushing them to be quiet.

The creature's arms flailed as its tentacles whipped about and its tail swung in wide arcs. Much of the air attack was thwarted, but the torpedoes hit their mark—the geyser of water at the thing's torso a clear indication. The beast roared and swayed in the water. It had been caught off guard again. More missiles were fired and more got through as the creature worked to right itself. It took direct hits to its jaw, head, chest and arms.

As the planes came around to unleash another onslaught, the creature turned toward the warship.

"Shit," Stoddard said. "It's got eyes on the ship."

"We need to get its attention back," Jeffries said.

Missiles sailed, the white trails filling the sky like cars in desperate need of an oil change. The creature spun to meet the attacks, tentacles intercepting. Winged serpents took flight and joined in the fray, sacrificing themselves and blowing apart like sacks of gelatinous rubber.

The behemoth spun back in the direction of the ship and swatted at a number of the ship's missiles using its lobster-like claw, the appendage seemingly indestructible. But the torpedoes were direct hits below the surface. The creature roared again as the white foam churned with purple. A few missiles got through, and the armor along its shoulder shattered where contact was made—the pieces flaking away like crust from a pie. A small, jagged hole formed, purple blood oozing forth.

Cheers and excitement broke out over the comms.

"Keep it up, men. We're going to take this sucker down," Jeffries said.

Stoddard felt good too, but not overly so. He only had a few missiles left. They needed the planes from the incoming carrier to get here fast.

The squads circled around again and would launch another attack in moments. The ship was holding off on firing, not wanting to attract the monster's attention more than necessary. Then without warning, the creature dipped below the waters.

"Damn it," Stoddard yelled.

"Shit," Jeffries said. "It went under. I repeat. The creature has gone under. Lost visual."

"We've got it on radar," the ship reported.

"It's probably going to come at you from below," Jeffries reported. "You've got to get out of there."

Stoddard, along with everyone else, knew there was nothing the ship could do, short of hurting the creature enough with torpedoes that it changed its course. But that wasn't going to happen. Yeah, they'd wounded it, but how much, no one knew.

"Don't count us out yet," the ship said.

Two LAMP IIIs, heavily armored helicopters, took off from the ship. They carried missiles and torpedoes.

"Lost radar contact," the ship reported.

"It's gone deep," Jeffries said, and everyone knew what that meant.

Time seemed to stand still as everyone, both in the air and on the ship, waited to see if the monster was going to come back. The silence was beyond eerie. Stoddard could've sworn he heard his heartbeat echoing off the cockpit glass.

A few minutes later, the ship declared it had made contact again. The creature was inbound.

"Contact," the operations officer said.

The monster was coming in fast, like a rocket launched from the bottom of the ocean, and directly below the ship's position.

A barrage of torpedoes was launched. With nothing left to do, the ship's crew braced for impact, hoping the weapons would stop the creature.

# CHAPTER 16

The behemoth saw the tiny weaponized objects coming toward it as it swam to the surface, and pulled up short. Tentacles shot forth, striking the torpedoes. Explosions riddled the waters, the impact forceful, but nothing more than an annoyance to the creature. A few of its tentacles blew apart, but the damaged appendages were quickly drawn into its body through the orifices from which they had come, while other tentacles emerged, ready to take their place.

With the threat gone, and before another attack could launch, the creature shot forward. It stopped just before coming in contact with the ship, realizing it didn't need to breach the surface in order to destroy the heavily weaponized thing and risk its welfare from the flying humans.

Its tentacles, both octopus and squid-like, broke the surface and slithered around the ship. It tasted human blood as each teeth-lined sucker mouth bit into flesh. The creature tightened its grasp on the ship and crushed it in multiple places, the steel crumpling like tinfoil in human hands.

The vessel was then yanked under and torn apart. Tentacles snatched up bodies, both alive and dead, devouring the tiny meals.

\*\*\*

"Holy shit!" Jimenez yelled.

"Did you see that?" someone else asked.

Stoddard opened his mouth to respond, but like the rest of the air fleet, he was stunned into silence. His heart pounded as his flesh lined with a cold sweat. He couldn't believe it. Two ships and their crews were gone, taken down in seconds.

The creature wasn't going to be stopped today, not with what they had available. And if more ships arrived, more people would die.

"That's it," someone said. "We need to get the hell out of here."

"Screw that," Jimenez said. "We need to kill that thing."

"I agree," Stoddard said, finally speaking. His voice sounded wary. "But not at sea. We're in its territory. We need to bring it to land."

"And how in the hell are we supposed to do that?" someone asked.

Stoddard thought it was Franklin, a lieutenant from the fourth squad.

"We get it to chase us," Stoddard said, not knowing if his idea was completely ridiculous or a good one."

"We aren't doing shit." Jeffries said, his voice sounding like a teenager in the midst of puberty, "until I hear what our orders are." He cleared his throat. "So for now, pipe down, keep your eyes peeled and stay in formation."

Stoddard had never heard Jeffries sound so frightened, but he had to respect the man for staying strong and speaking up, letting everyone know who was in charge.

The squadrons continued to fly around, remaining a good half mile above the ocean. Silence allowed Stoddard and the rest of the men too much time to think. Stoddard's mind went to his family and friends. Both groups gave him hope, but at the same time, they caused him grea despair. He might never get to see them again.

Finally, word came in from Washington, D.C. The fleet of aircraft was ordered to return to the states and land at Stewart Air Force Base, located about seventy miles north of New York City. It was the closest military installation to their location that would be able to house the pilots and deal with the large number of planes.

"We're giving up?" Jimenez asked.

"Yeah, Lieutenant, that ain't right," Stoddard said, knowing it was the correct thing to do, but wanting another go at the creature.

Others agreed, stating their displeasure at having to run from a fight. Though the men were scared, they all wanted vengeance for their lost brothers and sisters, but it appeared they weren't going to get it today.

# CHAPTER 17

With the warship destroyed, the behemoth came to the surface, hands loaded with crushed rock. It heard nothing except the water cascading off its huge body and the whipping of wind past its ears. Glancing around, it saw only cloud-dotted blue skies. The humans were gone.

The creature brought its arms down and smashed the water with its fists. It had wanted to finish the battle; destroy the humans and let them know they couldn't stop it. Keep them from alerting more of their kind. Now, they would return in greater numbers.

As its anger diminished and it began to think, it remembered that the humans could communicate across great distances, similar to how it could communicate with its winged serpents when they left its body. Having the humans escape made no difference, for their kind, back on land, were surely aware of its existence.

As the behemoth remained there, peering into the distance in hopes of seeing something—the speck of an aircraft, another ship—it felt a great sadness pierce its heart. The agony of its past came on strong, colliding with it like a tidal wave. It faltered, as if struck. The misery racking its mind was worse than any physical pain, a fresh wound refusing to heal.

It temporarily forgot about the present. The battle was a distant memory. Its body grew heavy. Its hands opened and the rubble fell free, back down into the murky depths of the sea. Then it too sank beneath the waters and descended slowly, like a skydiver after opening a parachute.

It hated the pain its human part brought with it. Nothing seemed to help except anger and hate. Those human emotions were the most powerful and overrode all others.

It thought of Vinnie. Saw the vile human standing before it. It saw Vinnie's subordinates, evil men who did his bidding with great pleasure. Those men had done the actual killing, but Vinnie was responsible, the man behind the curtain.

The creature's anguish quickly evaporated as rage filled its heart. It felt better. Its focus—vengeance—had returned. It had a mission and would see it through. No amount of physical pain, emotional angst or human weapon would stop it. Vinnie and his counterparts would be killed if it was the last thing it did.

The behemoth hated its human emotions, wanted them gone so it could just be a mindless beast of the ocean. It would then live at depths no human could reach. Be at peace while it lived out its life. That's what it wanted, but it had no idea if such a thing was possible. It had a mind, thoughts and feelings.

Even with its human emotions present, it could still choose to live a peaceful existence at sea. Maybe the anguish it felt would fade over time. It could hide from the humans until they forgot about it, until it became nothing more than a myth.

Hide? Never!

It needed to quench its thirst for vengeance. No amount of time would make it feel whole again, make it forget about its former life, family. It would never fail to remember Vinnie. The man's image had been branded onto its heart and into its mind, never to be removed until its demise.

The behemoth had been given life after death. The human part of it allowed to exist, to remember. It had a purpose, a second chance. Vengeance, the reason it had been reborn. The pain would never completely go away, would never stop hounding it, but if it killed those that had wronged it, it might feel a sense of peace, for it and its former loved ones.

Killing a single human in order to bring it harmony seemed so trivial and ridiculous, but none of that mattered. The dead would have their justice. Its human emotions would drive it forward and lead it to victory. All creatures—human or otherwise—that got in its way would perish under its wrath.

For a moment, it thought past the death of Vinnie and asked itself what would it do once the human was no more? It had thought it would return to the sea, live out its life, but it couldn't be sure it could do that. Live alone? Be by itself with only its thoughts to plague it? How could it survive like an animal if it wasn't fully one?

The behemoth shook its head. It couldn't worry about such human things now. It needed to focus on one thing and one thing only—revenge. Hopefully, killing Vinnie was going to be the one act that would give it peace.

It needed to find him, find . . . New York City.

The part of the behemoth that was human had once dwelled there. The metropolis was home to millions of humans. The creature wondered how to go about finding New York City without alerting them. They roamed the seas and skies. They would see it coming, find it and hunt it. It would do battle with them, that it knew, but it needed to make sure Vinnie was dead before that happened, or at least before it died. Until that time, it needed to be cunning, and to stay hidden.

Refocused, the creature swam to depths where sunlight could not go, where only ultimate darkness existed and where hideous creatures like itself, but smaller, dwelled, with their bulbous eyes, dark bodies and long sharp teeth—images that would make humans run in fear.

The creature then decided what it had to do and released a large number of winged serpents. They spread out and headed in different directions, all in search of New York City. They were not to engage any humans and were to report back with their findings as soon as they saw land. This would take time to accomplish, but in the end, it would be worth it.

# CHAPTER 18

As the serpents drew farther away, the behemoth lost its telepathic link to them. It did not worry, knowing they would return to it, like the faithful pets they were. They were a part of it.

The behemoth continued to gobble up meals, both minute and large, from tiny clown fish and lobsters to larger sharks and whales and the giant tubular worms that protruded from the ocean floor.

Swimming around in the tranquil seas without fear was not good for the warring creature. Time wore on and it grew bored, restless. Needing to wreak havoc, it tore apart the ocean, smashing miles upon miles of reef, floors and leveling underwater mountains. It needed to stay fresh and angry. It allowed itself to dwell on its past, on its family and let the pain of that time sink in and fuel its wrath. Let the hurt fester like an infected wound.

It fought with itself not to breach the surface as it waited for its serpents to return. Ships, with their noisy engines and obnoxious fuels that poisoned the sea—its home—could be heard from miles away.

Though it seethed with the need to kill and wreak havoc, even on humans that had nothing to do with it, it held itself in check and remained hidden. It continued to dwell on the things that haunted it, eagerly awaiting the return of its faithful servants.

\*\*\*

The serpents found land in every direction they went. Ships reported seeing strange creatures, winged sea snakes the size of automobiles, things from tales of old, from the time of myths from before man set sail across the Atlantic Ocean. Some people grew wary of the sea, sailors who'd been doing so for years. Others, who had never been on a ship, went out looking for the creatures in hopes of filming, capturing or killing them, for there were too many reported sightings for it to be completely false.

Videos started showing up across the internet, glimpses of giant-sized, scale-laden beasts, slithering about the sea. Not one shot was clear, all able to be dismissed as sick whales, tricks of the light or simply doctored. And with all the sightings, not one ship was attacked or person killed, leaving many to suspect it was all hype.

Of course, the United States military had video of the behemoth, and took the giant serpent sightings seriously. The president and his brain trust decided the threat was global and that all nations should be alerted. The monster videos from the battle—certain formations and fighting patterns deleted—were distributed quietly to other countries.

Every video on the internet was looked at with extreme scrutiny, utilizing the most up-to-date video equipment known to man. The fact that the behemoth hadn't been seen, and no ships had been reported missing or found destroyed, gave the military hope that the serpents were all that was left of the behemoth. Hopefully, the huge monster had died at sea from injuries it had sustained during the attack.

Eventually, the behemoth-battle videos were leaked onto the internet. For the most part, the public didn't want to believe they were authentic, until the government confirmed the threat.

People still went looking for the serpents and the behemoth, the seas full of craft. Military from all nations were put on high alert, ready to strike hard and fast should the creature show itself again. Fighter planes were at the ready. Tanks and missile trucks took up positions along shores and submarines and warships patrolled the coastlines.

Along with being scared, the entire world seemed eager for the thing to show itself.

# CHAPTER 19

Weeks passed before the first serpent returned to the behemoth. Within an hour, others arrived, with more following over the next couple days, reattaching themselves to the monster and relaying their findings by way of telepathic images. The creature saw everywhere its serpents had traveled, as if it had been to those locations itself.

While the winged snakes were absent, the behemoth had produced more. Now, there were twice as many slithering around its much larger body.

The creature became more and more frustrated with each returning serpent, the images of New York City it held in its mind not matching anything it was receiving. Then, to its pleasure, one of the serpents returned and showed it what it had waited so desperately to see. It recognized the landscape, the tall buildings, the busy waterways, airways and the familiar smells and sounds. The foggy, distant memories of the human it had once been came roaring back, and then it knew how to find the metropolis.

It felt a tingle come to life in its loins that spread across its body like a wild fire. It understood this emotion, knowing it was a human condition known as excitement. It was eager and . . . happy? Yes, joyful at knowing it was closer to finding Vinnie, and that its plan had worked.

Now it could move out and go to war, but like all battles, might wasn't the only component the winning side relied upon.

The creature was smart and would use its human intellect to achieve its revenge.

# CHAPTER 20

Stoddard and his entire fleet had been assigned to Stewart Air Force Base, located approximately seventy miles north of New York City. The airport was commercial too, but that section had been immediately shut down after the sea monster attack was reported, allowing the base to operate fully as a military installation.

Stoddard, his fleet along with another, had been at the base and on high alert since returning from their battle with the behemoth. He was able to phone his wife and let her know he was out of harm's way. He didn't know when he would be returning home, and with the creature's whereabouts unknown, he couldn't even give her an approximate date.

The entire eastern coastline of the United States was guarded by warship, plane and submarine. Nothing was getting through without being spotted, let alone killed or severely damaged. Countries all around the globe were on high alert, but only ones with superior militaries truly felt safe.

Stoddard didn't think the creature would come to land. Why would it? The sea was its home, where it ruled. Actually, he wasn't sure if it had originated from the ocean. Maybe it had come from another planet, some alien sent to wipe out the human race. He laughed at himself for imagining such a movie-like scenario. Then again, nothing was too "out there" to really believe.

The creature could have gone deep and found the ocean's depths more suitable, a place it wouldn't be bothered by humans. It might emerge now and again, there might be stories of missing ships, and it might take a plethora of them to go missing before the military took an offensive approach instead of the defensive one they were taking. Maybe, it would attack a Navy ship again, such an occurrence would surely get the brass stirring. They would want to hunt it down at that point.

There was the chance that the creature had died from some kind of infection sustained during the battle. It could have also returned to where it had come from, some other dimension or planet.

The truth was, Stoddard, along with everyone else, had no idea what had happened to the creature. But he did know that if it wandered close to shore, it would be lit up by an incredible amount of firepower, maybe even nuked. If nuked, it would surely die, along with whatever people were around it. Stoddard hoped it wouldn't come to that. The best bet was that the behemoth would take so much damage that it didn't want to bother with humans anymore. It would return to the deep sea where it was safe and far away from human presence, having learned to fear humans like so many other species on the planet had.

The serpent-sightings were odd though, because the winged beasts had been spotted by a number of ships. Reports came in from around the globe. If the behemoth was dead, then they had most likely scattered and were simply living out their lives or looking for a new place to dwell.

Of course, it was also odd that not one of the things had been clearly caught on video, captured or killed, and how the sightings had all come on or around the same couple days. Then, there were no more eyewitness accounts, as if the winged serpents had disappeared.

Stoddard hoped never to see the gigantic creature again, for the sake of people's lives, but at the same time, he also wanted to kill the thing, the primal need for vengeance still burning in his gut.

In the meantime, he could only stay at the ready, so he kept busy with mundane things—catching up on television shows, movies and playing an incredible amount of card games.

\*\*\*

From a special command post off the shore of Virginia, something large and moving fast showed up on radar. The thing was the size of two football fields. The operations officer made a call and the image was soon visible across multiple screens of various military vessels. The president was alerted and immediately airlifted to a secure location after it appeared the object was heading for Washington D.C.

Within minutes, fleets of air and sea craft were en route to the area from surrounding states. There was already a large contingent of military weaponry in and around Washington D.C., but the government wasn't going to take any chances, wanting the behemoth taken out as quickly as possible. Allowing it back out to sea was not going to happen.

Inland, tanks and missile trucks were at the shore, with more coming in from North Carolina and Virginia. Drones were launched and set out to sea. Apache and Blackhawk helicopters, armed with incredible firepower, hovered in the skies. Stealth bombers took flight and were en route, ready to drop their explosive cargo should the need arise. The world would be watching, and the United States of America was going to show it wasn't a nation to mess with, regardless of the enemy.

\*\*\*

Within minutes of the sighting, word had spread to all military installations in the country. News crews also got wind and almost every channel cut into their regularly scheduled programs. Stoddard, and everyone else on base, seemed to stiffen at hearing the announcement. A moment later, the mess hall was a cacophony of noise, as excitement levels reached new heights. Gone were the quiet games of chess and checkers, cards being flipped and pilots complaining about being cooped up. They didn't want to sit still. They wanted to join in the fight with their brethren, but would have to wait for the call and remain on standby.

The fight was far away, Stoddard knew, and there was already enough firepower there to destroy the behemoth a hundred times. He and his squadron would most likely not be needed and would remain on the sidelines, like bench players—suited up and ready to play, but only permitted to watch the game unfold.

Stoddard's squad had been in the shit with the monster, had lost fellow Navy men and women. They deserved to have another go, to strike back and bring the beast down. But orders were orders, and their base, being so far out, meant they were bystanders this time around.

Televisions were brought into the mess hall as news crews— the crazy people that they were—had set up remote cameras along the coast, waiting for action. The screens were filled with vast shots of the ocean, some broadcasts switching back and forth between actual pictures to radar images of something large off the coast, the thing only showing up as a green blob.

\*\*\*

The object on the radar screen had come in fast, but then remained about a mile from shore. Planes flew over the area, hoping to get a visual, but the beast remained submerged. Ships were told to hold near the shore. Subs, too. The objective was a defensive one for now, knowing that to follow it to deep waters was foolish. Finally, the order was given to fire long-range torpedoes, hoping to enrage the creature to attack. But just before the missiles hit the target, the object on the screen broke apart, like a swarm of gnats scattering after they were swatted at. Then upon closer examination of the radar images, it was realized that the object hadn't been a single entity but a huge gathering of smaller entities, like a school of fish grouped tightly together to fool predators into thinking it was larger than it was. The smaller marine life swam in different directions, going out to sea and deep, until their images vanished off the screen, leaving everyone baffled and somewhat relieved.

\*\*\*

The behemoth had known the humans would guard their cities. They would be waiting for it to show. It remembered New York

101

City as being of great importance to the humans, a crucial city to their way of life. When it arrived outside the area, it saw a number of stationary ships off the coast.

It's ruse of sending an army of its serpents elsewhere had hopefully worked. The humans had attacked the serpents, it knew, so the time to strike was now. It could only hope that they'd diverted most of their war machines to that area, leaving New York City with less protection. It would strike hard and fast, kill Vinnie and his men, then return to the sea.

From a few miles off the coast of the northeastern seaboard of the United States, the behemoth stood on the ocean floor, unmoving, and sent a small contingent of the winged serpents to take care of and report on the humans' defenses outside of New York City.

*** 

The *USS Camouflage*—one of the Navy's experimental submarines—was the lead ship, its captain in command of the fleet off the shores of New York City.

"Sir," the Camouflage's radar man said. "We have incoming."

"What is it, Fellows?" the captain asked.

"Not sure, but according to our scanners, the objects appear organic and rather large, whale-size."

The captain knew about the large winged serpents. Hell, everyone did.

Zooming in on the radar screen, they appeared like squiggly lines. "Serpents, like the ones down in D.C."

"They're coming right at us, sir."

According to reports from D.C., the scaly creatures had scattered when attacked, disappearing back into the ocean depths. He wasn't going to take any chances. These things were on a direct course with each sub, as if in attack formation.

"Alert all water craft," the captain said. "I want defense measures taken and weapons fired. They'll most likely run off. They haven't been aggressive, yet, but I'm not taking any chances."

The orders were given and relayed across the waters.

"Sir, there's no way we'll be able to get them all."

"Let's hope the things retreat, and if not, then we pray and brace for impact."

\*\*\*

Explosions rocked the waters off the coast. Serpents exploded, the sea becoming a mixture of purple ink-like clouds and chunks of serpent flesh. But only a small number had been taken out. Some had only been wounded, with gashes along their bodies and holes in their wings.

Each sub could only defend itself. There was no craft spared from an incoming attack. Before the last torpedo detonated, the serpents had reached the submarines' exteriors and the ships' underbellies, latching onto the thick hulls with their sucker mouths.

The Camouflage activated one of its defensive measures called SHOCK, a maneuver that electrified the exterior of the craft with 100,000 volts. It was designed to stop enemies from boarding and fry any kind of enemy-attached surveillance equipment. Two serpents that had reached the sub were killed before they had a chance to breach the hull.

The rest of the fleet wasn't so lucky. The creatures secreted their acid-like substance and quickly ate through the thick steel. The serpents then made their way into the crafts, spewing more acid throughout the interiors, but also munching on crew members, filling their bellies with human meat. The subs and ships took on water. Men's and women's screams echoed throughout as alarms continued to blare uselessly.

"We've got four incoming," the Camouflage's radar man said.

Torpedoes were locked on and fired, taking out the giant slithering snakes. But more were approaching from ahead and below. Torpedoes were fired again. The serpents came in fast, one exploding only twenty feet from the sub, rocking it. The Camouflage was holding its own, taking out incoming serpents with torpedoes and electrocuting any that managed to attach themselves to it. The experimental craft proved a formidable foe against the creatures, but the rest of the fleet was gone, ships sinking, crew dead or dying.

When the battle was finished, the Camouflage was the only remaining vessel from the fleet that had been assigned to guard the northeast coast.

\*\*\*

The behemoth remained at its location, watching from afar through the serpents' eyes. All the craft had been destroyed save for one. The thing proved different, powerful, as it defeated any and all winged beasts that attacked it. But the slithering winged creatures had done their duty and performed well, making way for their master to move in.

Staying glued to the ocean floor, the behemoth crept along, as the remaining sub continued to battle the serpents, the smaller creatures a wonderful distraction. Just as the behemoth drew beneath the ship's position, the last of its serpents were defeated. If the humans had seen it, they hadn't let it know. No weapons were fired at it.

The behemoth sprang from the ocean floor, its course set, target locked in its sights.

\*\*\*

The sub's radar picked up an extremely large and rapidly moving blob, the thing appearing as long as a midtown skyscraper.

"Incoming," the radar man yelled.

The captain's mouth fell open and he ordered torpedoes to be fired. Both men hoped it was a school of the serpents, but the advance radar system identified the object as a single life form, with multiple life forms gathered on it, and they knew it was the monster from the videos or one just like it.

"I want nukes readied," he added. "But hold on my orders."

\*\*\*

The behemoth saw the torpedoes racing toward it and shot out its tentacles to intercept the weapons. The detonations were powerful, blowing apart the ends, but causing no severe damage. Shockwaves washed over it, doing little to rattle it, but letting it know the weapons were different from the ones it had encountered before. Another wave of torpedoes followed and one got past its defenses, exploding against its right shoulder. Its carapace shell protected it, but the impact was felt, like a giant hand pressing down.

Another attack was launched and another torpedo got through. The behemoth was struck in its lower right rib area, where its armor met and a line of soft flesh was exposed. Pain shot into the monster, the beast feeling as if it had been skewered by a flaming lance.

The behemoth realized it was taking too much of a defensive tactic, instead of simply attacking the sub with the ferocity and rage it had used on the humans before.

Like a charging bull, the creature shot forward. More torpedoes came at it, but it took them out with the precision of a neurosurgeon, sacrificing its numerous appendages as it sailed through the foggy waters.

It reached the sub and grabbed hold with both hands, ready to tear the boat apart, when it felt white-hot, electric pain radiate up its arms and spread across its entire body. The creature couldn't move, its muscles in a spasm.

Then the jolting pain ceased, but its body still pulsed with discomfort.

The sub fired torpedoes from its rear, the underwater missiles arching around and slamming into the behemoth's back. It roared in surprise and pain.

Then the white-hot, electric pain returned and it couldn't move, its hands seemingly cemented to the ship. Its teeth gnashed together and it bit its tongue. Finally, the electric pain stopped. Then more torpedoes launched from the sub and hit the behemoth in the abdomen and legs, ripping apart exposed flesh. The wounds were small—no serious damage yet—but if the attacks kept up, the injuries could worsen.

The humans were hurting it.

Wishing it could shove the entire submarine into its mouth and devour it along with the entire crew, it decided to release the ship from its grasp, having learned that the object was too dangerous to hold.

Its anger was now rage. More torpedoes were launched, but this time, along with its plethora of tentacles, it released its winged serpents, the sudden congregate of beasts like a flock of seagulls taking off. Torpedoes were intercepted or blocked, the detonations barely coming into contact with the behemoth. It swung its lobster-clawed tail around and swatted the submarine. The front side of the underwater craft crumpled, but the steel remained intact as the vessel went twirling away, but not before torpedoes had been fired again.

The behemoth was struck in its starfish orifice, one projectile managing to make it a few feet inside the beast where it detonated. Like a thousand bee stings, burning, needle-like pain burst across its center. Serpents that had been inside, gestating, were obliterated. The behemoth closed the chest mouth as its facial maw roared. Its tail shot out and the claw closed around the center of the submarine, jerking the craft to a sudden stop.

The creature felt the white-hot pain race up its tail and it howled in protest. Determined, it fought through the spreading agony and clamped down. The claw crushed the metal, splintering it, breaching the interior, and then, with a final squeeze, cut the underwater vessel in half. The pain caused by the sub immediately ceased and the behemoth knew it had won.

Reaching out with its hands, it took hold of the two halves, then sent its thinner-sized tentacles into the sub and searched through the hallways and into rooms. It plucked dead and dying humans free. The diminutive meals were barely crumbs, hardly chewable, but chewed it did, making sure to taste every last human soul.

When it was finished, it kept the two halves of the sub in its grip and headed for the surface. It was time for war.

# CHAPTER 21

Stoddard's regime got the call for action. He and his fellow pilots were in the air minutes later and heading to New York City, where the creature had taken out the entire Navy fleet of watercraft.

He never truly thought he'd get called into action against the monster. Not after hearing about what was happening off the coast of Washington D.C. and even before then. He had imagined the creature would show up at some point, but nowhere close to where he would be. Maybe on the other side of the globe. The fact that it had come to the U.S. was a complete surprise. He and the others had wanted another go at it, and their wish had come true. But now that reality was unfolding, he, along with the others, knew it would have been better for all if the thing had died at sea or simply vanished. There had already been too many deaths, and after the catastrophe off the shores of New York, the number had substantially grown.

None of that mattered now. He and his men were going to get another chance at killing the creature. For some, it would be their first time battling against it.

During the flight, he, along with Jeffries, Jimenez and others that had fought the behemoth, told what they knew and what to watch out for. Jeffries was the air mission commander and went over protocol on formations and attack patterns, again, having already done so when they were stationed at the base.

A large part of the military had not only been placed near and around Washington D.C., but a lot of the other forces had gone there after it was thought the creature had been offshore. But it had only been a grouping of its winged serpents, the things almost like servants, obeying the creature's commands. Stoddard had seen them in action, seen them maneuver and commence in surprise attacks, as if they had been working with the behemoth instead of simply acting like animals and attacking or fleeing. They had also given up their lives, acting as shields to protect the beast.

There had been talk that the serpents showing up off Washington D.C.'s shore had been a diversion by the monster. Stoddard certainly thought so, which made it clear to him that the beast was able to think and plan. It was now more dangerous than ever. But it also meant that it shouldn't and wouldn't be underestimated.

The armada of fighter planes tore across the sky, rattling windows and setting off car alarms on the streets below. They reached the metropolitan area in minutes. The waters surrounding the city were chaos. Ships were sinking. Flames licked the air. Black smoke filled the sky. Winged serpents were fluttering about, picking off the few sailors still alive. There was no one left to save at sea, only the creature to kill.

Then Stoddard saw it, the colossal creature that had killed so many people. Its head broke through the surface like a whale coming up for air. Its shoulders and torso soon followed as it marched toward the city. It was soon standing, the water up to its waist. The creature had something in its hands, and it took Stoddard a moment to realize it was the halves of a submarine.

"Ay Dios Mio," Jimenez said. "That ain't the same thing we fought. It got bigger."

"It looks like it's heading straight for the city," someone said.

"All right, men," Jeffries yelled. "You all know the drill. Now let's drop this fucking thing."

The behemoth reached back an arm and threw one of the halves of the sub. Quick thinking pilots fired missiles, as the destroyed vessel tumbled through the air. The wreckage was blown apart into fragments that cascaded across the West Side Highway and into buildings. Pavement was gouged, brick crumbled from buildings along with glass from shattered windows. A few pedestrians were mauled and sliced in half or crushed. Vehicles, both parked and driving, were hit with debris and damaged. A box truck tipped over after a large piece of the sub crashed into it.

The beast roared in protest and tossed the other half of the sub. Missiles were fired from the wave of fighter planes. The sub was hit, the back end blown apart, but the rest remained whole. The chunk of sub crashed into two buildings, the structures bursting upon impact and sending a bombardment of concrete and glass over the crowded sidewalks and clogged streets. People screamed from fright and injury. Blood splattered the scene and body parts littered the sidewalks. The buildings then crumbled under the half sub's weight like a flattened sand castle, the sediment like a wave as it splashed over vehicles and covered a section of the roadway.

Stoddard felt his blood run cold. His stomach churned with unease and disbelief. Then like a spark igniting dry brush, anger blossomed within him. His nostrils flared. He needed to scream, and did. Other men did the same, swearing and crying out.

After the din of outrage faded, Jeffries spoke up. He reminded the men that they had a job to do, and that no matter what they witnessed, what happened, the beast needed to be stopped. It was time to rely on training and to focus the anger they felt. There were millions of people on the ground, and there would be catastrophic casualties if the creature made its way to land. It was now time for all out war.

As the behemoth drew closer to shore, its thick muscled legs rising in and out of the water caused huge waves to crash against and over the coastline, washing away debris, cars, trucks and people.

Planes flew in from all sides, locking on areas of the beast, trying to target its head and softer parts. Missiles were fired. Tentacles lashed out, along with serpents. Explosions riddled the air around the beast, few weapons getting through the monster's defenses.

Within minutes, more fighter planes arrived from another base. The air was a sea of organized chaos, squads flying in unison, launching wave after wave of attack. The behemoth didn't slow, didn't seem fazed by the different weaponry that hit it. It moved forward, not attempting to go after any of the planes, as if they were nothing more than annoying flies, not even worth swatting at.

Sirens echoed around the city. Police, fire and ambulance units were responding to the overwhelming amount of calls received by the 911 operators.

Missile trucks stationed along the city's shore launched Patriot missiles in conjunction with the fighter planes' attacks. Tanks fired their shells, but the projectiles only bounced off the behemoth like spitballs. The air was filled with a mixture of the ear-splitting sounds of war, black and white smoke and a feeling like the world was coming to an end.

More and more attacks were getting through, the creature's carapace armor holding strong, but the softer flesh areas, including the neck, showed signs of damage. The purple flesh glowed brighter, like irritated skin, and trickles of its fluorescent blood flowed like the streams of some alien river. The scene gave the fighting men and women hope, but seeing the creature continue forward and disregard the attacks was also discouraging.

Then, as if hearing the thoughts of the combatants, more tentacles came forth and took up the defense, along with the winged serpents, the scaly, onyx-purple colored beasts bursting like blood-filled balloons. They were coming from the monster's starfish-shaped cavity in droves, as if the behemoth were fulfilling a heavily demanded holiday order.

The creature had reached the city, but before stepping onto the island, the eel tongue came from the mouth and sprayed the shore with its acidic venom. The portion of coastline vanished, along with the missile trucks and tanks, cars and any structures in its path, leaving a sizzling foam behind. It then stepped over the bubbling mess and onto the West Side Highway, crushing vehicles and fleeing pedestrians. Due to its massive weight, crevices opened up below its feet and spread outward, like cracks of lightning, and swallowed vehicles, people and small buildings. Car alarms sounded throughout, adding to the already noise-saturated air.

The behemoth roared in victory, the eel tongue lashing about like an angered cobra, but spitting no more venom. The creature stepped into the city, leaving behind crater-sized impressions in the pavement below and tearing down three buildings in its path. It swung its arms, pulverizing more structures, sending brick, concrete and citizens across the city. Its tail whipped side-to-side, taking out more man-made constructions.

Fighter planes continued their assault, but now that the creature was surrounded by buildings filled with citizens. That, along with its defenses, made attacking the monster much more difficult.

A missile got through and hit the behemoth square in its nose. It let loose a roar as purple blood dotted its mouth. It reached down, tore into the street with its claws, taking vehicles, waterlines, and people with it, then threw the debris at a squad of incoming planes. The pilots hadn't been expecting the crafty attack. The rubble came on too fast and ripped the entire squad apart, easily shredding the group of metal craft like a giant-sized shotgun blast.

Another squad came in from the north side. Missiles were fired. The eel tongue lashed out and spewed its orange-colored venom. The missiles disintegrated along with the squad behind them.

The creature's reach went farther than originally thought, as if it was saving the attack for when it needed it the most, and wanting the element of surprise.

The behemoth marched forward, knocking down everything in its path, leaving behind a trail of wreckage and chaos. Fires sprang up all over from ruptured gas lines. Water was flooding the streets from burst water mains. Bodies lay in droves. Many of the survivors were wounded, suffering from crushed arms and legs from falling debris. Fingers and other body parts lay about, floating away down the sewer like leaves after a storm. The sharp coppery scent of blood was thick in the air.

Fighter planes had to fly closer to the beast now, or they risked hitting the surrounding buildings. The attacks were mostly coming in from behind now. Jeffries didn't want to chance more casualties, but if they didn't stop the creature, there were going to be many more regardless.

Serpents were fluttering about, creating a fog-like shield around the creature, making it even more difficult to strike. Some flew at the planes, coming close enough to cause them to divert their course. Machine gunfire from the aircraft came into play, the bullets able to pierce the hides of the winged serpents.

No one understood why the behemoth had come onto land and wondered where it was heading. Maybe it was attracted to something biological. Either way, it needed to be stopped before it erased the city from existence. But it was taking less damage now, as if it was using the buildings as shields.

"Just got word from command," Jeffries said. "They're thinking about firing nukes at it."

"That's crazy," Jimenez said. "The city . . ."

"Millions will die," Jeffries said. "I know."

"We can't let that happen," Stoddard said.

"No shit," Jimenez said.

"But what are we supposed to do?" someone asked.

"For now, we keep hitting this thing and hope we can stop it before a nuke is launched," Jeffries said.

# CHAPTER 22

The creature remembered the city, remembered where its home had been. It knew the way, its eyes and the eyes of its winged brethren showing it all the nooks and crannies of the metropolis. It worked its way through the city, toward the Hudson River, where it would have to cross. It would be out in the open there and more vulnerable to attack again. It had taken damage, wounds opened along its body now. The buildings were protecting it, but its tentacles and winged serpents were being torn apart. It had hundreds of both, but the numbers were dwindling. The humans were proving more powerful than it had imagined they would be. It would need to return to the sea where it could eat and replenish itself, heal.

The behemoth was all right for now, its injuries many, but insignificant. Pain was only a feeling, and the ache it felt from its loss, from Vinnie, was far greater than any physical angst the humans could cause it.

When it reached the Hudson River, the serpents flew into the open first. The creature scanned the area as it continued to defend itself from incoming air attacks. It saw the humans and their weapons along the opposite shore.

The behemoth stepped into the river. Waves shot up and splashed over FDR Drive, flooding it and the streets around it. A barrage of weapons launched from the Brooklyn Bridge off to the creature's right. Missile trucks and tanks fired their payloads.

The behemoth lunged in the bridge's direction, coming close enough to reach out and swat the pesky humans. It faced the historic landmark and opened its mammoth-sized mouth. The eel tongue shot out and spewed its orange venom. Support wires snapped. Metal melted and brick dissolved. Humans disintegrated. Weapons exploded, sending molten fragments in all directions. Along with the continuous air assault, missile trucks and tanks along the Brooklyn side of the river continued to fire.

The behemoth glanced toward the shore, and as it did, brought its tail around and clobbered the bridge, crushing what remained and bringing the entire thing down, where it splashed into the river. It then spewed its toxic venom across the coastline, dissolving the shoreline—grass, park benches, trees and the line of military vehicles. Surviving soldiers ran about, many with missing limbs and burned flesh, only to stumble a few seconds later, dead, nothing but a smoking pile of goo.

A group of fighter planes came in low under the Manhattan Bridge and fired missiles, the attacks now aimed at the creature's legs. The behemoth batted the attack away with its tail, then snatched at the rising squad of fighter planes. Two were hit, their wings clipped. The planes went spiraling away and crashed into buildings that hadn't been touched by the behemoth.

The creature moved forward, stepping in long strides and was on Brooklyn soil in moments, bringing hundreds of gallons of water with it that washed away much of the melted mess at its feet. It knew where to go, saw the serpents' path. They had found Vinnie's home.

*** 

Vinnie's henchmen had also been discovered. The vile humans had been at a bar called Lou's, a place they frequented. The behemoth let his serpents have the men for themselves, for the human scum were just pawns. It wanted the man in charge, Vinnie.

Four serpents surrounded Vinnie's mansion before two of them stormed in, crashing through windows, one via the garage and one through the front door, the heavy oaken wood splintering like kindling as the serpent crashed through and wedged its way past the frame, stretching it out. They found him and his family in the large living room. Vinnie fired his handgun at the creatures as they slithered in, but the bullets couldn't penetrate the hides. His wife was snatched up, along with his two children. Vinnie cowered in a corner as the creatures hissed, his wife and kids wrapped up in python-like style. They screamed and begged for him to help, but he only whimpered, begging for his life. Then the serpents slowly squeezed the life out of his family and he had to listen to their screams of pain, then the crushing of their bones and the popping of their organs.

He sat scrunched up in the corner, tears streaming down his cheeks, his pants piss and shit laden. He wondered why the creatures weren't finishing him off, the agony of waiting too much to bear.

\*\*\*

The behemoth continued to strike out against the attack on itself. Its hide was tough, but faltering in places, the damage adding up. There were cracks in its armor now, its flesh exposed and bleeding. It had less and less to use to defend itself. The serpents were few and many of its tentacles were too short to intercept incoming attacks due to the damage they had taken. The human assault was relentless, like a poked and prodded beehive.

The need for vengeance was too great for it to care about itself. Seeing through the serpents' eyes, hearing what they heard, it could taste revenge, the *human condition* wickedly delicious. They had saved Vinnie for it, kept him from escaping, and made his suffering great by hurting his loved ones, killing them slowly.

The physical pain racking the behemoth's body was forgotten; its steps picked up, hurried. It practically ran, crushing apartment buildings, homes, people, cars and anything else in its path.

When it reached Mill Basin, it saw the ocean beyond, the sight filling it with hope that once it was finished, it could return to the sea and leave the human world behind.

It stood over the mansion, barely able to fight off the incoming aerial assault from above, its tentacles all but finished. Then, using its thinnest of tentacles—having saved it for this moment—it extended it into the home. The appendage found the living room in seconds. The serpents backed away as it moved in and coiled the tip around Vinnie's ankle, then dragged him outside.

\*\*\*

Stoddard couldn't believe what he was seeing. All the chaos and destruction and the creature just stopped. It didn't seem to care about being hit anymore, as if its concentration was on the house. They continued to fire upon it as the behemoth pulled a man from the house and held the dangling morsel in front of its face. If the creature inhaled too deeply, the human—like a speck of dust—would be gone. It stared at the person, its head tilting ever so slightly from side to side, like a dog watching the outside world through a living room window.

"What the hell is it doing?" someone asked.

"That's exactly what the Pentagon wants to know," Jeffries said.

"Are we supposed to stop, sir?" Jimenez asked.

"No, but they want to know who it's holding."

"This thing gets weirder and weirder . . ." someone said.

As great as the want to know what the creature was doing, the goal was to stop it, bring it down, so the attacks poured on.

\*\*\*

The behemoth continued to ignore the pain riddling its body and secured its catch by wrapping it up in a thicker tentacle. There was no way it was taking a chance its prey would be harmed or killed by anything other than itself.

Wanting a moment to relish its revenge, the behemoth reached down and scooped out chunks of earth, ripping out waterlines and cement, and hurled the debris at the planes, hitting a few and causing the rest to scatter.

Given a few moments of peace, the behemoth brought Vinnie before its eyes. It ground its teeth, jaw muscles bulging. It wanted to communicate, let the wicked human know why it was there for him. But it could not speak, couldn't even fully comprehend its human characteristics, but it knew it needed to kill this man in order to ease its pain.

The tentacles slithered up Vinnie's leg like rapidly moving creeper vines and encompassed his body in seconds, leaving only his head unobstructed so the monster could relish in his screams.

The suckers along the tentacles attached themselves to Vinnie, then began to eat. The teeth-lined orifices devoured the man's flesh slowly, the behemoth wanting the man to feel every bite. He screamed in pain, spittle flying from his lips, eyes bulging in terror and disbelief. Muscle was removed, fat and tendon too, leaving just enough flesh around the man's torso for him to remain alive, even if only for a few more moments. Blood covered the behemoth's tentacle, the sucker mouths trying to lap it all up. The meal was but a crumb, but the beast savored it, tasting every cell.

With blood bubbling from Vinnie's mouth like the foaming of a rabid dog, his screams gurgled sobs, the creature opened its mouth and flung the dying human inside, then swallowed him whole.

Vinnie was gone. Dead. No more.

The behemoth felt no different, had no sense of satisfaction. The pain radiating in its heart was still there, as present as ever. It didn't understand.

Pain began riddling its flesh again as the human attack resumed. Its time to relish was over. It needed to react, to protect itself, to fight back. But it couldn't move. It didn't understand why its internal angst wasn't gone. It just didn't make sense.

Frustrated, it stomped the ground like a spoiled child that doesn't get his way. If the pain wasn't going to leave it, then what was it supposed to do? How could it live with such hurt? It had no idea where to go or what to do and bellowed a cry that shook the nearby houses' foundations and set off every car alarm in the area.

It staggered as its legs took solid hits from three missiles. The behemoth managed to catch itself before falling. It was a bleeding, oozing mess of wounds and sores. It wanted to die, to let the humans have their revenge for all the devastation it had caused. It was evil like Vinnie, had killed so many in its path to revenge.

It couldn't meet its end this way. There had to be more to its existence than this. A reason it was made to be, had been allowed to live . . .

The behemoth pushed itself up, got its feet under it and rose. It knew what it had to do, the idea hitting it like a punch to the gut. The weight of its actions caused its legs to wobble, but it didn't go down. The reason for its existence was so obvious now. It had a lot to make up for. Maybe never would be able to. But it would try. The humans might never accept it, forgive it, but that didn't matter anymore.

Its rage and sorrow were gone, as if shaken off, like water from a dog after a bath. A new type of energy and exuberance filled it, despite the condition of its battered body. It needed to leave. To hide. Disappear for a time. Let things die down. Then it would keep watch over the humans. It would be their protector. Do something good, for its past life human life, as well as its current one, were awful. Dark spots on humanity.

A moment later, it took off running, jumping into the bay, trudging through the shallow waters, avoiding any craft it saw. The planes followed it, hammering it with their weapons, but it accepted the pain. It had prodded the bees' nest and deserved its sting.

When it finally reached the open sea, it dove, and followed the ocean floor's descent, going deeper and deeper where the sun's rays refused to travel and the humans were another world away.

There, the behemoth remained, eating, healing and living. Years later, it would return to the surface periodically, keeping an eye on the mortal world, making sure they were protected from things like itself, should there ever be any others.

# THE END

# CHECK OUT OTHER GREAT KAIJU NOVELS

## MURDER WORLD | KAIJU DAWN
## by Jason Cordova
## & Eric S Brown

Captain Vincente Huerta and the crew of the Fancy have been hired to retrieve a valuable item from a downed research vessel at the edge of the enemy's space.
It was going to be an easy payday.
But what Captain Huerta and the men, women and alien under his command didn't know was that they were being sent to the most dangerous planet in the galaxy.
Something large, ancient and most assuredly evil resides on the planet of Gorgon IV. Something so terrifying that man could barely fathom it with his puny mind. Captain Huerta must use every trick in the book, and possibly write an entirely new one, if he wants to escape Murder World.

## KAIJU ARMAGEDDON
## by Eric S. Brown

The attacks began without warning. Civilian and Military vessels alike simply vanished upon the waves. Crypto-zoologist Jerry Bryson found himself swept up into the chaos as the world discovered that the legendary beasts known as Kaiju are very real. Armies of the great beasts arose from the oceans and burrowed their way free of the Earth to declare war upon mankind. Now Dr. Bryson may be the human race's last hope in stopping the Kaiju from bringing civilization to its knees.
This is not some far distant future. This is not some alien world. This is the Earth, here and now, as we know it today, faced with the greatest threat its ever known. The Kaiju Armageddon has begun.

# CHECK OUT OTHER GREAT KAIJU NOVELS

## KAIJU WINTER
by Jake Bible

The Yellowstone super volcano has begun to erupt, sending North America into chaos and the rest of the world into panic. People are dangerous and desperate to escape the oncoming mega-eruption, knowing it will plunge the continent, and the world, into a perpetual ashen winter. But no matter how ready humanity is, nothing can prepare them for what comes out of the ash: Kaiju!

## RAIJU
by K.H. Koehler

His home destroyed by a rampaging kaiju, Kevin Takahashi and his father relocate to New York City where Kevin hopes the nightmare is over. Soon after his arrival in the Big Apple, a new kaiju emerges. Qilin is so powerful that even the U.S. Military may be unable to contain or destroy the monster. But Kevin is more than a ragged refugee from the now defunct city of San Francisco. He's also a Keeper who can summon ancient, demonic god-beasts to do battle for him, and his creature to call is Raiju, the oldest of the ancient Kami. Kevin has only a short time to save the city of New York. Because Raiju and Qilin are about to clash, and after the dust settles, there may be no home left for any of them!

www.ingramcontent.com/pod-product-compliance
Lightning Source LLC
Chambersburg PA
CBHW070755120626
46557CB00002B/607